McKenna, Ready to Fly!

by Mary Casanova

★ American Girl®

For the kids and volunteers at the Forget-Me-Not Riding Center,
for young gymnasts everywhere,
and for readers of all kinds and abilities.
Follow your dreams!

Published by American Girl Publishing, Inc.
Copyright © 2012 by American Girl, LLC

Questions or comments? Call 1-800-845-0005, visit americangirl.com, or write to Customer Service, American Girl, 8400 Fairway Place, Middleton, WI 53562-0497.

Printed in China
12 13 14 15 16 17 18 19 LEO 10 9 8 7 6 5 4 3 2 1

Illustrations by Brian Hailes

Photo credit: p. 122, David Harpe

Real Girls stories adapted and reprinted from *American Girl* magazine

Special thanks to Jeanelle Memmel; Patti Kelley Criswell, MSW; Dr. Laurie Cutting; Dr. Debbie Staub; Dr. Nissa Peterson; and Dena Duncan of Three Gaits Therapeutic Horsemanship Center

Cataloging-in-Publication Data available from the Library of Congress

Contents

Like butterfly wings, a hum of energy filled the gym at Shooting Star Gymnastics. Then I realized that the hum was coming from me! After more than two long months, my broken ankle had finally healed. My cast was coming *off*!

Friday.

Only *three* days away.

Waiting to take my turn on the uneven bars, I could hardly sit still on the mats beside my level-four teammates. I happily wiggled my bare toes at the end of my cast, which was covered with a zillion signatures.

Coach Isabelle tucked her sleek brunette hair behind her ear and scanned our team of ten girls. Then she nodded to Sierra Kuchinko, sitting on my right. "You're up next, Sierra," Coach said.

With her red hair pulled back in a loose ponytail, Sierra hopped up and approached the low bar. Because of her extra height, she jumped up with ease—unlike some of my teammates, who needed a boost. Although Sierra was new to Seattle and our team last fall, she'd made steady progress. She muscled through her routine with a smile.

"She's getting really good!" I whispered to Toulane Thomas, who was sitting on my left. Toulane and I have been "gym rats," practicing gymnastics together, since preschool.

Between Toulane's intense dark eyes, a tiny gully of worry formed. "Maybe *too* good," she said, lowering her voice. "My mom said there are only two open spots on the competitive team. Sierra might grab a spot that should be yours—or *mine*."

Toulane glanced at the viewing area, where her mom, Mrs. Thomas, sat and watched with eagle eyes. Ever since Toulane's older sister, Tasha, was injured and had to quit the competitive gymnastics team, Toulane had been getting all of her mother's attention—maybe too much, because under her mom's watchful eye, Toulane couldn't seem to relax.

"Don't worry," I said to her. "March-fest and tryouts are still two months away."

March-fest was a big event—a day when Shooting Star's competitive team would compete with other area gymnastics clubs. For Toulane and me, it was also the day when we would try out with other girls to be on the level-four competitive team. I studied my cast. *I* was the one who should be worrying about tryouts, not Toulane.

Toulane wrapped her arms tightly around her knees. "But the stakes are extra high this year with only a couple of spots available," she said, raising her hand to chew at a fingernail. "I just feel all this pressure. Don't you?"

I nodded. I *was* worried about team tryouts, but now that my ankle was nearly healed, I couldn't wait to throw myself back into training.

"This comes off Friday," I whispered back, tapping my cast with a grin.

"Finally!" Toulane said, a little too loudly. "Then we'll be a real team again."

Coach Isabelle held her finger to her lips and nodded toward the bars, reminding us to focus on our teammate's routine. As Sierra swung through to her dismount, I held my breath, hoping she'd stick her landing. But she came down wrong and fell to her knees. I could see the disappointment in her face, but she jumped up quickly and shrugged it off.

"Nice overall routine, Sierra," Coach Isabelle said, writing something on her clipboard.

"Good job!" I said, smiling over at Sierra as she dropped down onto the mat beside Toulane. I couldn't hold it against her that she was *good*. Plus, she'd become a friend.

I absolutely couldn't *wait* to get back to doing what I loved.

To gymnastics.

To soaring again.

A thousand butterflies took flight inside me.

The next afternoon, I glanced outside the school library windows at the drizzle coming down. On the glass, beads of moisture formed into tiny rivers. But inside, it was warm and cozy as Josie and I worked together. Josie had started tutoring me last fall, when I'd been struggling with reading. At first I met with Josie twice a week, but now we're down to once a week, and our time together always flies by.

Blue paper snowflakes twirled slowly overhead as the clock neared three-thirty. I started stuffing my backpack with books, ready to head home.

But Josie wasn't packing up. She twirled the ends of her blonde hair with one hand and tapped the arm of her wheelchair, which she'd nicknamed "Lightning," with the other.

"What's up?" I asked. "Is something wrong?"

"I'm scared," she said, dimples playing at the edges of her strained smile.

"You? Scared?" I asked. It was hard to imagine anything flustering Josie. She may not have full use of her legs, but Josie makes up for it with her sky-high grades, her flute-playing ability, and the way she's always helping others. "Scared about what?" I asked.

"Horseback riding," she answered in a small voice.

"Horseback riding?" I repeated. "Seriously?" I tried to picture Josie balancing on horseback, but I couldn't.

Josie nodded. "At a therapeutic horseback riding center," she explained. "I asked my mom if I could try horseback riding, and she said okay. But now I'm in a panic. I mean, I want to ride, but what if I fall off?"

I was worried about Josie falling, too, but I couldn't tell her that. "Well," I said, "I can't imagine they would let you ride unless it was safe."

"Yeah, I guess," said Josie, dropping her gaze to her lap.

I didn't know what to say next. I didn't want to see Josie fall and get hurt, but I didn't want her to miss out on something that might be lots of fun, either.

"Josie," I said, leaning closer and whispering, "in gymnastics, every time I try something new, I get scared, but I try not to let that stop me, y'know?"

Josie's eyes flickered with uncertainty.

I hoisted my backpack to my shoulder and stood, pointing to my cast. "This thing comes off soon," I said. "When I start back at *full* routines, I'm sure I'll be scared—afraid I'll fall and get hurt again. But I have to try."

"But you're going back to something you used to do," Josie said. "I've never been on a horse before."

I hesitated. She had a point there. Then I had an idea.

"Hey," I said, "if you'd like, I'll come with you to the riding center."

"You will?" Josie asked brightly. "Really?"

I nodded. "You've helped me so much," I said. "I'd love to help you."

"That'd be great!" Josie said, beaming.

"When are you going?" I asked, zipping up my jacket.

"This Friday," she said, "right after school."

Uh-oh. Josie looked so happy that I didn't have the heart to tell her that my doctor's appointment—when this cast would finally come off—was the same afternoon. Could I find a way to do both?

———★

Grandma Peg picked me up from school, the

way she'd been doing ever since I got my cast on in November, and we headed in her red Jeep to Almost Home—Mom's coffee shop.

We stepped inside, setting off the brass bells above the door. *Ting-ting, ting-ting.*

"My favorite visitors!" Mom said from behind the counter. She was wearing her red apron, as usual, with a button that read: *Coffee Cures the Winter Blues!*

"Homework, McKenna?" Mom asked.

"Nope," I said, propping my crutches against the counter and sitting on a stool. "I finished it today with Josie."

Mom leaned across the counter, a dangly earring sliding out from beneath her sandy hair. She placed her hand on top of mine. "Good for you, honey!" she said. "To celebrate, how about a vanilla steamer and a peanut butter cookie?"

"Sure," I said. *My favorites!*

Grandma Peg left us at the counter, calling over her shoulder, "I'm going in back to check on the twins."

Mom poured a small pitcher of milk, added a squirt of vanilla, and pushed it under the stainless steel nozzle. *Hiss!* The milk frothed and steamed. Then she poured it into a yellow mug, sprinkled cinnamon on its foamy cap, and set it in front of me, along with a cookie. *"Voila!"* Mom said with a grin.

"Thanks!" I said, warming my hands on the mug. "Mom? Is it okay with you if I go with Josie this Friday to a horseback riding center? It's for kids with disabilities. I think she could use a friend."

Mom reached for a rag to wipe down the counter. "What time?" she asked.

"Right after school," I said.

"But, McKenna, what about your doctor's appointment?" she reminded me. "It's all you've been talking about lately—counting the days until you can get your cast off."

"I know," I said, taking a sip of my steamer. "But I was hoping, maybe, somehow I could do both?"

Mom shook her head. "Pretty tough," she said. "Maybe you can go with Josie another time?"

I hesitated, picturing Josie's anxious face earlier in the library. "I want to get the cast off, Mom— I really do," I said. "But Josie needs me on Friday. I don't know what to do."

"Do you want me to try to reschedule your doctor's appointment for next week?" Mom asked.

I shrugged uncertainly.

"Think about it for a while, and we'll figure

something out," Mom said.

I nodded, swallowed my last bite of cookie, and then carried my steamer to the back room of the shop. I sat down beside Cooper, the world's best dog—not because he's such a cute golden-doodle, which he is, but because he's mine. He stretched out on his back as I stroked his curly coat.

Maisey and Mara, my twin five-year-old sisters, were cuddled up in the easy chair with Grandma Peg as she read aloud to them.

Legs outstretched on the rug, I stared at my cast. I needed it *off*. And I needed every single day between now and team tryouts in March if I hoped to make the competitive team.

But Josie had done so much to help me get back on track with my schoolwork. Thanks to her, I wasn't falling behind any longer. Going to the riding center was one big thing I could do to show her I cared.

I made a decision. I stood back up and headed out to tell Mom.

"I said I'd go with Josie," I said, leaning across the counter. "And I don't want to let her down."

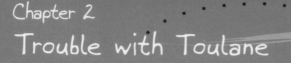
At gymnastics on Thursday, I stretched with my level-four group in a big circle on the mats, doing whatever moves I could with my cast on. I was easing down into the front splits. Beside me, Sierra's legs flattened out into side splits. None of the other level-four girls had her flexibility! Sierra's legs made one long pencil.

"Sierra, you must be made of bungee cords," I joked.

She laughed, her hair brushing the mat. "You'll be passing us all as soon as you get your cast off," she said.

Mom had rescheduled my doctor's appointment for Monday, but now I was second-guessing my decision. I could have had the cast off *tomorrow*. Just thinking about it made my skin itch under my cast.

I took a deep breath and slowly exhaled. *Josie is worth it*, I reminded myself. Just a few more days of waiting. Plus, I was curious about the riding center and looking forward to seeing it with Josie.

"Guess what, Sierra," I whispered. "I'm going to a horseback riding place tomorrow."

Toulane overheard me. "Tomorrow? I thought you were getting your cast off," she said. "Isn't that what you told me?"

"I *was,* but I moved that to next week," I said.
I saw disappointment flash across Toulane's face, so
I tried to explain. "I offered to go with Josie because
she was scared. She needed a friend."

Toulane's face soured. "You make it sound like
you and your tutor are best friends or something,"
she said, her voice suddenly sharp.

"We *are* friends," I said. "So what?" I didn't get
it. Was Toulane jealous of my having a new friend?

Toulane sat up straight and tall, still in her
splits position. "You're a *gymnast,* McKenna," she said.
"And you're really good, too. You don't have time to
add other sports—and lots of new friends."

"I can be friends with whoever I want,"
I snapped back.

The rest of our team froze in position, as if
waiting to see what would happen next.

Just then, Coach Isabelle stopped talking with
one of the other coaches and stepped back to our
circle. "Girls, you're supposed to be stretching, not
arguing," she scolded. "Everybody up. Change of pace.
I want you to get a look at the rhythmic gymnastics
class that's starting at the club. It's different from what
we've been doing in artistic gymnastics."

We followed her to the gym's east wing. I lagged

behind, clunking along with my crutches and feeling anything but graceful. When I finally made it to the studio, I sat down on the last empty chair—by Toulane—and stretched out my leg in front of me.

As the instructor demonstrated a floor routine with a gold-and-silver ribbon, she pulled me in like a magnet. Her movements were part gymnastics and part ballet, and the ribbon swirled overhead as if it had a life of its own. Then she demonstrated other rhythmic events—the rope, hoop, club, and ball.

Toulane and I sat side by side, not speaking, but I could tell that she was interested in rhythmic gymnastics. Her eyes were glued to the instructor.

As the instructor picked up the gold ribbon again, she paused and asked, "Now, do any of our visitors want to try?"

I was a little stunned when Toulane leapt up. "I do!" she said.

The instructor handed Toulane a purple ribbon. "Just follow my moves," she said.

As if Toulane had spent hours practicing, she gracefully followed the instructor's moves. Toulane was a natural—and she smiled the whole time. I couldn't remember the last time I had seen her looking so relaxed and happy.

"Wow!" I said to Toulane when she sat back down. "That was amazing!"

"Thanks," Toulane said, her face flushing. "I used to do rhythmic gymnastics at summer camp. I loved it! I wish I could take this class."

"Maybe you could," I suggested.

"No way," Toulane said with a sigh. "My mom thinks I need to stay focused on making the competitive team."

"You should at least *ask* your mom, Toulane," I said. "You're really good—I mean that."

Toulane said nothing, but she gave me a quick smile. Then she chewed her lip, as if considering what I'd said.

After about twenty minutes of watching, Coach Isabelle led us back to the bars. "It's great for you guys to get a look at other forms of gymnastics," she said. "But now it's back to practice."

Toulane was up on bars first, still wearing her smile from rhythmic gymnastics. As she whipped around the low bar, I had to admire her speed and energy. But at the dismount, she flew from the bar much too fast. She sped forward through the air, completely missing her footing, and landed flat on her chest. She hit the mat with a groan. "Ummpph!"

13

Coach Isabelle stepped forward, ready to help. But Toulane quickly pulled herself up to her knees, her eyes flashing. She slapped the mat with one hand.

"Want to try again?" asked Coach Isabelle.

Toulane shook her head, avoiding Coach's eyes. She stood and walked away from the bars.

Before Toulane could sit back down, her mom, Mrs. Thomas, hurried over from the viewing area.

Uh-oh, I thought. Parents aren't supposed to come out on the mats.

From the mat's edge, Mrs. Thomas scolded Toulane. "If you want to be a competitive gymnast," she said, "you can't quit that easily, Toulane. You need to get up on that bar and try it again."

Coach Isabelle cleared her throat. "Mrs. Thomas—" she began.

"I'm sorry," Mrs. Thomas interrupted. "I know one coach is enough. I just want her to do her best." With one last meaningful glance at Toulane, she walked back to her seat.

As Toulane adjusted her ponytail, she blinked back tears. Sometimes I wondered if she was a gymnast because she *wanted* to be or because she felt she *had* to be.

I glanced at the viewing area, caught Grandma

14

Peg's eye, and waved. She waved back. Grandma Peg
comes to every practice, just as Mrs. Thomas does.
But I never feel pressure from Grandma to be the
best gymnast. I know that no matter how well I do,
Grandma loves me just the same.

As I stood at my locker after practice, I saw
Toulane and her mom walking toward me. A poster
for the rhythmic gymnastics class hung on the wall
along the edge of the gym. Toulane hesitated in front
of the poster and then said a few words to her mom.

Mrs. Thomas's response was short and loud.
I heard the words *time* and *money*. When Toulane
stepped up beside me to open her locker, her face
clouded over.

"Did she say no?" I asked gently.

Toulane nodded. "But she's right," she said
in a strained voice. "If I really want to make the
competitive team, I have to stay focused. There's no
time for things like rhythmic gymnastics—or horseback riding," she added pointedly.

I didn't even have a chance to respond before
Toulane pushed her locker door shut and walked
away, her jaw set in a determined line.

That night after dinner, Dad and I walked Cooper, who loved stopping by every bush, tree, and crack in the sidewalk along the way. That was fine, because I wasn't moving that fast anyway. With my cast wrapped in a plastic bag, I clomped with my crutches around the block. It wasn't raining or drizzling, but a faint mist hung in the air.

"So how was your day?" Dad asked.

"Good," I said. "But I can't wait to get this *rock* off my leg."

"Mom said you put off your doctor's appointment by a few days so you could help Josie tomorrow afternoon," said Dad. "Is that right?"

My foot suddenly itched, and I wanted to rake my fingernails under my cast. "Yeah," I said, still wondering if I'd made the right decision. Toulane's words at the gym had shaken me.

"You're a good friend," Dad said.

"Thanks. But that's not what Toulane would say," I added.

"Why?" asked Dad, pausing for a moment to let Cooper sniff a bush. "What's Toulane saying?"

"That I've lost my focus," I said. "That I'm spending too much time on other things."

Dad stopped and put his hand on my shoulder.

He looked at my cast and then cracked up laughing. "You? Unfocused?" said Dad. "That's pretty funny. You never miss practice, not even when you have a cast on."

I didn't laugh, but I liked the way Dad helped me feel better about myself.

"Don't worry, McKenna," he said. "You'll get your strength back and be amazing again at the gym before you know it. And when you do, Toulane will probably complain that you're getting *too* far ahead. You think?"

"Sounds about right," I said.

Dad squeezed my hand, and we set off again.

When we passed the neatly trimmed hedges in front of my classmate Elizabeth Onishi's house, I waved, just in case she was looking out the window. We passed other dogs and their owners and several bicyclists, and Dad said "hi" to everyone. We walked up to the neighborhood park and down again, past the warm lights of old two-story houses.

When we returned home, I hung up my scarf and jacket and then tried to walk quietly through the living room toward my bedroom. Mom was on the couch, sound asleep. No wonder she was tired. She's at the coffee shop by 4:30 every morning!

I wanted to get a jump on the next chapter in my science textbook. I still wasn't the strongest reader in fourth grade, but I'd made progress. Mr. Wu, my teacher, wasn't worried anymore that I was falling behind in class, but I still knew that the harder the subject, the longer it took me to read it.

In my bedroom, I settled into the chair at my desk, tucked under my loft bed like a cozy cave. On the shelf beside my desk, Polka Dot, my brown and white hamster, scampered around and around on her wheel. Near my feet, Cooper settled onto his bed with a huge sigh.

"Was your day pretty hard?" I teased.

He wagged his tail.

"Napping, eating, chewing rawhide, taking a walk—it's a tough life, isn't it?" I asked.

Cooper closed his eyes, looking perfectly content.

I turned to Chapter Nine in my science book and read aloud to myself, one paragraph at a time. I paid extra attention to the first and last sentences, which often make the main points.

I had learned from Josie to pause after each paragraph and to *visualize,* or picture in my head, what I'd just read. That kept me from daydreaming about something else. Visualizing my reading wasn't that much different, really, from going over my gymnastics routines in my head. Josie had helped me see that I had a strong imagination, and I could use it to help my reading just as I used it to help me with gymnastics.

I sniffed the air and wrinkled my nose. Something smelled terrible! "Is that why you're running, Polka Dot?" I asked. "I'd try to escape that cage, too, when it stinks that bad!"

A knock sounded on my door. Before I could say anything, Mara and Maisey bolted in. "Will you help us with our handstands?" Maisey pleaded.

"Will you spot us?" Mara chimed in.

First the cage, now my sisters. "I'm *trying* to do my homework," I huffed in irritation.

"*Ple-e-e-ase?*" the girls begged in unison. Sometimes I wonder if they practice that word together. When they join forces, it's hard to go against them.

I decided I could turn this to my advantage. "Tell you what," I said. "I'll spot you if you help me clean Polka Dot's cage, but not yet. I'll take a study break in twenty minutes. Deal?"

"Deal!" my sisters agreed, and then they bounded back out the door.

Exactly twenty minutes later, the timer buzzed in the kitchen. Feet pattered back to my room. This time, Mara and Maisey were in their matching pink dinosaur pajamas.

"Mara, you watch Polka Dot, okay?" I said.

She nodded.

"Keep her from going behind my dresser," I reminded her.

"I know, McKenna," said Mara impatiently. "I'm watching her."

Maisey and I emptied the old bedding from the cage into the garbage can. Then we took the cage to the laundry room tub and washed and dried it completely. From a large bag, we scooped fresh cedar chips into Polka Dot's cage, lining the floor.

"I love this smell," Maisey said.

I agreed. "So much better!"

Then we returned to my bedroom and set the cage back up with its wheel and food bowl in place.

Mara started giggling. "Polka Dot is tickling me!" she said. "She's up my sleeve!"

"Polka Dot," I announced, "your palace is ready!"

Mara leaned over the cage and shook out her pajama sleeve. I watched a bulge move down her arm, until Polka Dot slid out into the fresh chips below. She wandered around her cage, as if exploring a brand-new world.

"Okay, now I'll help you two," I said to my sisters. "Maisey, you first."

As my sisters took turns doing handstands, I spotted them, supporting them with my hands along their backs or up at their ankles. "You two are getting better and better, you know that?" I said.

It felt good to help my sisters. And my room smelled much better now, too.

When I turned back to my science chapter, my brain felt more awake. I'd learned that sometimes it's good to take a break from something difficult and return to it fresh. I put my visualization "powers" to work and pictured what I was reading. If I put my mind to it, I knew I could do it.

I hope that's true for gymnastics, too, I thought as I wiggled my toes outside my cast. *I hope, I hope, I hope . . .*

Chapter 3
Hearts and Horses

Under a steady rain, Josie's mom picked us up from school on Friday. I climbed into the backseat, where one bucket seat had been removed for Josie's wheelchair. Josie wore braces on her legs, and her arms were crossed tightly.

"Are you cold?" I asked.

She shook her head.

"Still scared?" I asked.

"Yup," she said. "But that's why you're coming along!" she added with a laugh.

I squeezed Josie's hand. I hoped I could offer her a little coaching in courage, but the truth was, I didn't know what to expect at the riding center either.

Mrs. Myers handed us a canvas bag filled with snacks and juice drinks. About 25 minutes out of Seattle—and after some serious munching on apples, cheese sticks, and chocolate-covered nuts—we turned onto a gravel drive under a log arch. The sign read: *HEARTS and HORSES. Riders of all abilities welcome!*

I noticed Josie reading the sign, too, and I elbowed her lightly. "All abilities, Josie," I said. "That means those who have never been on a horse, too."

Josie scrunched her shoulders up to her ears. She looked terrified.

Mrs. Myers found a parking space among

a few dozen vehicles. As the van door slid open,
I whispered, "Josie, breathe."

"Right," she said.

With the help of a hydraulic lift, Josie and her
wheelchair swung out of the van and lowered slowly
to the ground. I hopped out after her, my crutches
under my arms.

The outdoor riding arena was empty, but it
was raining, as usual, so I wasn't surprised. In the
distance, trees and hills framed a few fenced pastures
and a cluster of large buildings.

We hustled through the double doors of the
nearest building. From a red popcorn machine in the
corner of the lobby came the smell and sound of corn
kernels popping. Beside it stood a water dispenser.

"Well, hello!" a white-haired woman greeted us
from behind an office window. "I'm Irene. Everyone
signs in here first." Then she turned her gaze to Josie.
"And you must be our newest rider, Josie Myers?"

Josie whispered to me, "Gulp." But then in her
usual confident voice she said, "That's me!"

I felt extra close to Josie at that moment, knowing that she was allowing me to see her fears—the
scared part of herself that she didn't show everyone.
It felt good to know that she *trusted* me.

"Here are a few forms to sign," said Irene, passing clipboards to Josie and Mrs. Myers. "And visitors," Irene said, waving me over to a thick book, "sign in here."

When we completed our paperwork, Irene led us around the center. She showed us bathrooms, all handicap-accessible, and a huge, modern kitchen, which Irene said was designed for lots of cooks and potluck gatherings. Next, she walked us toward a wall of colorful riding helmets tucked into cubicles. "Let's find a helmet that fits, Josie," Irene said kindly.

With Irene's help, Josie tried on several helmets and finally settled on a metallic purple one. "How do I look?" she asked me, grinning.

"Ready for *anything*," I told her. "Purple's your color."

Then Irene pointed us toward a set of swinging doors. "That's the arena," she said. "Shannon, our director, is waiting for you in there. Have fun!"

———————★

The riding arena was a blur of activity. As I stepped inside, I instantly felt jittery, even though I wasn't going to be riding. The sand-floored arena was filled with half a dozen horses and riders of all ages.

Most of the riders had lots of help. One person led each horse with a rope, and two people walked on either side of each rider. That meant Josie wasn't going to be sent off alone on a galloping horse. *Phew!*

When I took a closer look at some of the riders, I sucked in my breath. One little girl's arm ended at her elbow. Another rider's back was curved like the letter C.

A part of me wanted to run back out the door. Then I remembered the day I'd first met Josie. I'd felt nervous and not sure what to say or do—until I got to know Josie better. Now, too, I just needed time to get used to what I was seeing and get to know the riders. I took a deep breath and kept walking.

Just inside the fence surrounding the arena, a teenage girl in jeans and red cowboy boots walked a small rust-colored horse with a flaxen mane and tail. It carried a blue-and-black-striped blanket and a silver-studded saddle, cinched around its wide belly.

As the horse neared us, Josie stopped her wheelchair beside the fence. "Oh, your horse is so cute!" she said to the teenage girl.

"She's a sweetheart," the girl agreed. She pulled a brown biscuit out of her pocket and handed it to Josie. "You can give her a treat, if you'd like—on the

flat of your hand, though, so she doesn't mistake your fingers for the treat."

Josie looked at the biscuit in her hand. So did the horse. With a soft nicker and sweet eyes, she stretched her head toward Josie.

"Like this?" Josie asked, extending her hand slowly.

With velvety lips, the horse found the treat, and it quickly disappeared.

"She loves treats," the teenager said. "You wouldn't know it now, but when we first took this horse in, she was rib-bone thin."

"That's *sad*," Josie said, stroking the horse's forehead. "But you're getting enough to eat now, aren't you, girl?"

Standing behind Josie's chair with Mrs. Myers, I giggled. "*More* than enough," I joked.

"Myers?" came a big voice.

"Right here," Mrs. Myers said with a wave.

Josie and I glanced up. From a wide platform, a woman with spiky blonde hair called, "Come on up!"

As Josie wheeled up the ramp with her mom's help, I headed toward the bleachers, where other people were watching the riders. "McKenna, where are you going?" Josie called after me. "I need you!"

I grinned and carefully climbed the ramp with
my crutches. Above the ramp, I noticed a huge board.
It charted names of riders, horses, side-walkers, and
leaders, plus days of the week and riding times. And
there was Josie's name, right next to "Pumpkin."

I wished Josie could ride the horse she'd just
met. What if this other horse wasn't as nice?

When I reached the top of the platform,
the blonde woman reached out her hand to me.
"Welcome!" she said. "I'm Shannon, and I'm helping
Josie get started here today."

She turned back to Josie and said, "You'll ride
for an hour, and with each ride you'll learn something
new. Riding's fun, but it's much more than that. For our
riders, it's a sense of motion. With each step the horse
takes, you'll be flexing and strengthening *your* muscles,
too. But first things first. Ready to meet your horse?"

"Okay," Josie said hesitantly.

Shannon glanced toward an open sliding door.
Beyond it I spotted several horses and ponies in stalls.
They were haltered and saddled, ready to go. But
Josie's horse came from the other direction.

"Halley! Bring Pumpkin over!" Shannon called
across the arena.

"Sure thing, Shannon," said the teenager who

was leading the rust-colored horse—the *same* horse that Josie had already met and fallen in love with! Josie and I exchanged an excited glance.

Holding the lead rope, Halley led the horse into the chute beside the mounting platform.

"Josie," Shannon said, "meet Pumpkin."

"Oh, we've already met!" Josie said happily.

"Great!" said Shannon. "And this is Halley, who'll be leading your horse today."

Halley smiled up at Josie. "This lead rope is attached to Pumpkin's halter," she said, "so you can just hang on to the saddle horn. You don't need to use the reins yet—unless you want to."

"And here are your side-walkers," Shannon said, nodding toward a couple as they approached.

The man looked as if he had just come off a cattle drive. "Howdy!" he said, smiling and tipping his worn cowboy hat. "They call me Cowboy Bob."

"And I'm his better half—his wife, Britta," the round-faced woman said. "We'll be at your side, with a hand on each leg."

"Thanks," Josie said. "But I don't know if I'm ready . . . "

Cowboy Bob gave her a reassuring wink. "You're going to do just fine," he said. "We'll be with you every step of the way."

His wife added, "The hardest part is deciding to get in the saddle. After that, it's easy as pie."

Josie's lower lip twitched. I knew the feeling. Sometimes trying a new element at the gym made me nervous, too. Then I remembered something Josie had told me when she first started tutoring me.

I leaned toward her ear and whispered, "Remember, one step at a time?"

Josie smiled and nodded.

"Well, you've already taken a few steps," I said. "You gave Pumpkin a treat and petted her, right?"

Josie nodded. "I guess so," she agreed.

"And the biggest step of all was deciding to come here," I went on. "I think that's really brave."

Shannon patted Josie's shoulder. "You'll enjoy riding Pumpkin," she added reassuringly.

Just then a teenage boy rode by on an Appaloosa with only a leader—no side-walkers.

"Hey, Logan!" Shannon called to him.

"Hi, Shannon!" the teenager replied, keeping his eyes on the arena ahead. Dressed in black from his cowboy boots to his helmet, the boy appeared completely at ease with his horse. He didn't grasp the saddle horn at all, but held the reins in one hand.

Shannon turned to us. "Bright guy," she said, "and a natural on horseback."

"What's his . . . ?" I started to ask.

"His disability?" Shannon said, reading my mind. "He's blind."

Josie shot me a look of amazement.

I closed my eyes for a moment, imagining what it would be like to ride a horse without being able to see. I didn't like using crutches, but at least my injury would heal. I felt a twinge of guilt, opening my eyes to gaze out at the riders whose disabilities may *never* get better. Then I noticed something. Beneath the many colored helmets, nearly every rider was *smiling*.

That gave me another idea. If Josie could only visualize herself . . . "Hey, Josie," I said. "Picture yourself riding Pumpkin with a big smile on your face."

Josie closed her eyes for a few seconds, and I saw the smile spread slowly across her face.

When Josie opened her eyes, Shannon asked, "What do you think? Ready to try?"

Josie drew a deep breath and smiled at me. Then she gave Shannon a nod.

Josie's mom and Shannon supported Josie as she stood up from her wheelchair. They each took an arm and helped Josie ease one leg over the saddle.

The moment she was seated upright on Pumpkin's back, Josie's shoulders began to rise.

"Hey, Josie," I said lightly, "your shoulders aren't meant to be worn as earrings." It's something Coach Isabelle often says.

Josie grinned and let her shoulders relax. "Thanks," she said, sounding more confident now.

Then she set off, with Halley leading Pumpkin, and Cowboy Bob and Britta on either side. Beneath her purple helmet, Josie was beaming. I watched until she made a full circle around the arena.

As another family arrived with their son, I headed to the bleachers, where Mrs. Myers was already sitting down to watch.

"Hey, McKenna!" a familiar voice called out from the upper bleachers.

I searched for the source of the voice and found, to my surprise, that it belonged to my classmate and neighbor Elizabeth Onishi. Her black hair fell to the shoulders of her green sweater, and her bangs skimmed her bright eyes.

"Hey, what are you doing here?" I asked.

"What are *you* doing here?" she replied.

I climbed to the top of the bleachers and sat

beside her. Then I explained that I was here with Josie, my tutor and friend. I pointed her out.

"And that's my brother, Julius," Elizabeth said, pointing to a boy whose curly hair stuck out from under his zebra-striped helmet. It almost matched his black-and-white-spotted pony. "He's my half-brother," Elizabeth said. "He's seven, but he has some special needs so he seems younger."

Julius was adorable. His expression was wide open and innocent as he talked with his side-walkers.

"He rides Oreo here every week," said Elizabeth. "He's wild about that pony."

"I didn't even know you *had* a brother," I said.

"That's because he lives with my dad and stepmom," explained Elizabeth. "I don't see him that often. That's why I come here. It's something we can do together. I look forward to it all week."

The next time Julius circled back toward us, Elizabeth waved Julius's side-walkers and leader closer. I followed her to the edge of the arena, and before I knew it, I was looking up into her brother's eyes. He glanced at me shyly. "Me Julius," he said.

"Hi," I replied. "I'm McKenna. Nice to meet you, Julius."

"Me too," he said, waving sweetly as the

woman leading his horse led him back into the circle.

"Elizabeth, spread the word, will you?" the woman called over her shoulder. "We need more volunteers, especially with the open house coming up!"

When I sat back down on the bleachers beside Elizabeth, I asked, "Volunteers?"

"There's always something to do here," she said. "Just ask Shannon or Cowboy Bob. Sometimes I help out on weekends with my stepmom."

While I watched Josie and Julius ride, I wondered, *Could I volunteer at the center, too?* I already had my hands full with school and gymnastics but was really enjoying my time at the riding center. Was there something more I could do to help out?

★

The hour flew by, and before I knew it, some of the riders were dismounting, including Julius.

"Bye, Josie," Elizabeth said as she left with her family. "Hope I see you next week!"

Soon, Josie was done riding, too, and she was all smiles. Shannon, Cowboy Bob, and Britta helped Josie dismount, while her mom steadied the wheelchair.

"I loved it!" Josie said.

"I knew you could do it," I said, feeling like a genuine coach.

As I walked down the ramp beside Josie, I remembered something. "Just a sec," I said to her, turning back toward Shannon, who was following us with Mrs. Myers.

"I heard you need volunteers," I said to Shannon. "Something about an open house? I might be interested . . . "

Shannon lit up and told me about the day when the riding center would be open to the public so that people could learn more about it. "We could definitely use your help getting ready for the open house," said Shannon. "When you come back next time," she said, "let's talk."

I nodded happily.

I had come to the center for Josie, but I was surprised by how much I'd enjoyed my time—once I'd gotten past my fear. As I headed on crutches out of the riding center, I reminded myself that I was *lucky*. Lucky to get my cast off soon. Lucky that my physical challenges were for only a short time. *Lucky* to have a friend like Josie.

Monday after school, I sat on the examination table as Dr. Hartley carefully cut off my cast, her eyebrows knit in concentration. The cast soon dropped from around my foot and ankle.

I looked at my pale skin and saw instantly how my calf muscle looked smaller—weaker—than my other calf muscle. Tears rose to my eyes.

I glanced at Mom, and her worried expression told me that she'd read my thoughts.

Dr. Hartley nodded at me. "Go ahead," she said. "Slip off the table and try it out."

I stepped down gently on my leg, but it didn't feel as strong as I'd hoped. My voice came out wobbly. "I thought I'd be . . ."

I couldn't finish the sentence. How could I possibly be ready for team tryouts in March? It seemed impossible—like climbing Mount Everest.

"McKenna, you're a gymnast," Dr. Hartley said. She squeezed my shoulder and then leaned over and looked me in the eyes. "You know all about hard work. Just start slowly, and build up your workouts a little at a time. And you'll start working with a physical therapist, too."

"When?" I asked.

"That's where you're heading next," she said,

making a note on the computer.

I left the office, still using crutches and gingerly putting weight on my cast-free foot.

At the physical therapy department, a young woman named Willow met me with a fist bump. "I heard you were coming!" she said brightly.

Willow asked me what my goals were, and when I said I wanted to make the competitive gymnastics team in March, her lips scrunched together. "That's not much time," she said, "but if you're willing to work hard—"

"Oh, I'm willing!" I said eagerly.

Willow put me on a schedule and gave me a sheet to chart my stretches and progress. "We'll be working on your range of motion, balance, and strength training," she began. "You may still want to use crutches for a while."

Then Willow showed me a few things I could do at home: calf stretches, ankle circles, and alphabet exercises. I liked those the most. With my leg supported, I pretended to draw the letters of the alphabet with my toes.

"I'm in fourth grade," I said as I formed invisible letters, "but I'm starting all over again with the alphabet."

Willow laughed, which made me laugh, too. For the first time that afternoon, I felt as if maybe things were going to be okay.

———————★

The week passed slowly, but I took every moment to stretch and strengthen my ankle. While I did homework, I made circles with my foot. While I watched a movie, I sat on the carpet and stretched my legs out in front of me, pulling a bath towel against the balls of my feet.

By Tuesday at the gym, I wanted to throw myself into a full practice, but I had to pace myself. I practiced balancing on one foot while the others started practicing floor routines.

After a minute or two, Toulane leaned in toward me. "Hey, I see you brought your tutor," she whispered. "Do you need her to tutor you in *gymnastics* now, too?"

I looked toward the viewing area, where Josie was sitting and talking with Grandma. Josie had come to the gym to watch, and then Josie's mom was picking us up after practice and taking us out to eat.

"She's not tutoring me here," I said to Toulane. "We're *friends*."

At the word *friends,* Toulane's expression turned stormy. She rolled her eyes at me and walked away.

"What's your problem, Toulane?" I called after her, a little too loudly.

Coach Isabelle overheard. "Okay, time-out," she said, holding her hands in a T shape. "Everyone take a seat for a moment."

I sat by Sierra—and as far away as possible from Toulane. Why did she care who I was friends with? Was she really that jealous of Josie?

Coach Isabelle took a deep breath and then said, "Lately I've noticed some tension between some of you girls." She glanced around the group, but I couldn't meet her eyes. I knew she was talking about me and Toulane. "Maybe we need to find a way to build a better sense of team. Any ideas?" she asked.

Breaking the silence, one girl said, "A sleep-over? We could watch movies and bring sleeping bags right here to the gym."

"Mmm," said Coach Isabelle, considering the idea. "Good suggestion, but I'd have to think about that one. I need my sleep, whereas I think you girls might want to stay awake all night. Am I right?"

A few teammates giggled.

"Any other ideas?" Coach asked.

I held up my hand.

"McKenna?" she said.

"There's a horseback riding center for riders with disabilities," I began. "They're looking for volunteers to help out. Maybe we could do something there on a Saturday."

A flurry of excited whispers rose up around me. "Horses, really?" someone said.

Another teammate added, "Cool!"

I risked a glance at Toulane, half waiting for her to shoot down my idea, but she said nothing. She had her arms wrapped around her knees in a tight little ball, her face frozen in an unreadable mask.

When I turned back to Coach Isabelle, her eyes were bright. "McKenna," she said, "I think you might have something there. I'll look into it."

I sank back into the mat, proud that Coach Isabelle was willing to consider my suggestion to volunteer at the riding center. Toulane obviously wasn't crazy about the idea, but I couldn't help that.

Soon our level-four group started stretching, and then we began the circuit around the gym to different pieces of equipment. With everything I tried, I felt shaky on my weak ankle. I finally sat down on the mat and blinked back tears of frustration.

"You know," Coach Isabelle said, kneeling beside me, "injured bones can heal and be stronger than before. Keep doing what you're doing. I'll work with you and keep track of your progress, okay? Just take things slowly."

I sighed. "But will I get strong enough by March-fest?" I asked.

Coach Isabelle shrugged. "Honestly, I don't know," she said. "But if anyone can recover from an injury, I believe it's you. One day at a time, McKenna."

Just then, Sierra ran like a gazelle at the mat stack and aced her vault.

"Nice work!" Coach called out.

Sierra bounded over to us. "Hey, McKenna," she said, catching her breath, "if you need any help with some of your exercises, just ask."

I loved that even though Sierra was focused on her own skills, she still made time to be a good friend. Steady gymnast. Steady friend.

———————★

By Thursday afternoon, I felt a little more sure of what I could try at the gym. And it helped knowing that Coach Isabelle was there to help, too. With each practice, I could work a little harder, but she'd make sure I didn't overdo it.

Before we got started, she announced, "Girls, I want you to take home these permission slips and get them signed by your parents. One week from Saturday, we'll work out here as usual, and then we'll take the team van over to the therapeutic horseback riding center. I called, and they would be *delighted* to have us come and volunteer."

"What are we going to do?" Sierra asked excitedly. She is always up for anything.

"We're going to use the riding center's kitchen to bake treats—for people *and* for horses—for the center's upcoming open house," Coach explained.

A murmur of excitement went up, especially about making horse treats. As the girls around me started chattering excitedly about the project, I caught sight of Toulane sitting in a far corner of the mat. Our eyes met, and she quickly looked away.

Part of me really hoped Toulane would go to the riding center. We needed to find a way to get along better, and volunteering together might be just what we needed. On the other hand, if she was going to show up at Hearts and Horses with a bad attitude, maybe it was better if she stayed home.

When Coach Isabelle invited me to try my bar routine, I forgot all about Toulane and the riding center. With my first hip circle, I felt a little bit stronger, a little bit lighter. Though I was far from flying through my routine, it felt good to be back in motion again, swinging in and out, up and down. When I neared the end of my routine, I held back from the dismount. Instead, I slowed to a stop and lowered myself to the floor.

With my floor routine, I held back, too. Without *strength*, it's hard to pull off *grace*. And I still needed time to rebuild strength.

Rather than risk falling off the beam, I used the floor-level beam, designed for beginners and for practicing new moves. At first I trembled, but I took it easy and paused several times to regain my balance and to calm myself. I kept my jumps low. I didn't need to go fast. I needed to rebuild my confidence one element— *one step*—at a time.

When I was done, I stopped to watch Toulane, who was working on her routine on the higher beam next to me. She flew through her elements, her forehead creased in concentration. When she dismounted flawlessly, her mom whistled from the viewing area. A faint smile crossed Toulane's tight mouth.

"That was really great!" I said.

"Thanks," she acknowledged.

And then I felt the need to say something more. I walked closer to Toulane. She had accused me of pulling away from her and from gymnastics, but that's not what I meant to do. We'd always been team-mates. That didn't need to change. "About the volun-teer thing," I said. "It's just one afternoon at the riding center. And I, um—I hope you'll come."

"You do?" Toulane asked, her intense brown eyes searching mine, as if she didn't quite believe me.

I nodded and said, "Of course!"

"Then . . . maybe," said Toulane. "If my mom lets me."

"You have to take a break *sometime*, right?" I asked.

Toulane's brow furrowed. "A break?" she said, glancing toward the competitive team. They were taking turns jumping into the pit—high and in per-fect form. As their coach, Chip Francesco, talked, he waved his arms in the air like a conductor.

Toulane's jaw clenched. "I doubt *they* take breaks," she said. "We can't either if we want to make that team."

Looking at Toulane now, it was hard to believe

she was the same girl I used to have fun with at the gym. When had she started to change?

"We're not *really* taking a break," I said to her. "We're team-building, remember?"

"I guess so," Toulane said, unconvinced.

As we left the mat, I wondered if maybe it wasn't Toulane who was changing, but *me*. What if I just didn't have the same *fire* about gymnastics that Toulane had? Was it wrong to care about other things, like the riding center, too?

I couldn't wait to return to Hearts and Horses. I'm not sure who was more excited—me or Josie! After working so hard toward becoming a better student, gymnast, and friend to Josie—plus encouraging my teammates to volunteer at the center—I felt so *good*. Stepping into the horseback riding center, a fresh breeze of excitement blew through me.

As I waited with Josie for Pumpkin to be led from the stable, Shannon introduced us to other riders as they passed. "That girl is a whiz at math," Shannon said, and, "That boy was adopted into a big family." The more I learned about the riders, the more I wanted to meet each and every one.

When a pink-helmeted little rider dropped her teddy bear near the mounting platform, Shannon let me step into the arena and pick it up. I handed it to one of the side-walkers, who lifted it to the little girl.

"*Tanks,*" the girl said, looking down at me. I'd seen her from a distance, but up close, I saw how everything about her face looked lopsided. Her right eye seemed fine, but when she turned her head and faced us, I saw that her left eye was much lower than her right.

I almost wanted to cry. *What if I'd been born looking so different?* I felt bad for the little girl, but she

didn't seem to be feeling sorry for herself. She gave
me a sweet smile.

I managed to smile, too. "You're welcome!"
I said.

"This is Dora," Shannon said, stepping down
off the platform to join us. "She's six, and she's been
riding here for over two years, haven't you, Dora?"

Dora gave me another lopsided half-smile. She
clutched the saddle horn so tightly that her fingers
and knuckles were turning white.

"Dora's a little nervous about letting go,"
explained Shannon. "We're working on ways to help
her relax."

I nodded—I knew something about that. In
gymnastics, Coach Isabelle is always trying to help us
relax and face our fears.

"Do you want to try my favorite trick, Dora?"
I asked her. "Take a deep breath in, like this—" I took
a deep breath.

Dora copied me, but she didn't loosen her grip.

"Okay, now let it out," I said, exhaling. Dora
did the same. "Nice job!" I said.

Then Dora did something unexpected. She
completely let go of the saddle horn with one hand
and reached over to mine, wiggling her fingers.

I wasn't sure what she wanted.

"She wants to touch your hand," explained Shannon.

I put my fingers up to Dora's, and then we held hands. Her little hand was soft and warm in mine. I felt myself melt into a puddle. "So, Dora, what's your favorite color?" I asked.

"Pur-ble," answered Dora. Her voice was high and sugar-sweet.

"Okay, purple. Good!" I said. "Now picture the color purple. Breathe it in, in, in."

Dora closed her eyes and breathed in. I noticed that as she did, her other hand relaxed a little on the saddle.

"Now, Dora, picture gray," I said. "Breathe out gray." I exhaled loudly, demonstrating for Dora.

Dora exhaled fast with a groan. "Oomph." It was funny, but in a cute way. From out of the corner of my eye, I saw that Josie was watching from the mounting platform. She was smiling, too.

"Okay, one more time, Dora," I said. "Purple in, in, in . . . and gray out!"

"Pur-ble in! Gray . . . OUT!" Dora said, shouting the last word. Already, Dora was sitting up a little straighter and clutching the saddle less tightly.

Shannon gave me a grateful smile. "Dora," she said, "can you repeat that while you ride?"

Dora nodded enthusiastically. Then she set off around the arena, punctuating the air every few paces with "Pur-ble in! Gray . . . OUT!"

I watched her ride away, and then I returned to the platform to see if Josie needed help. She didn't. This time she said she couldn't *wait* to get on Pumpkin's back. As she glanced toward the stalls, waiting for Pumpkin to enter the arena, Josie said, "So you met Dora? You were *really* good with her."

At Josie's praise, I felt a swell of pride in my chest. I scanned the arena and saw my new little friend sitting up straighter in the saddle, her pink helmet bobbing up and down.

When Josie set off on her horse, too, I searched the bleachers to see if Elizabeth was there. She was— two rows up from the bottom. She waved at me, a bag of popcorn in her other hand.

I was just sitting down beside Elizabeth when Cowboy Bob strolled past. "Girls, do you have time to help me with something?" he asked.

Elizabeth hesitated. "I would," she said, "but I promised my brother I'd watch him ride."

I jumped up. "I'll help!" I said.

Cowboy Bob's face, a road map of soft lines, stretched into a wide smile. "Thatta girl!" he said. He pointed to just outside the fence of the arena. Beside a wheelbarrow stood a manure fork with a red plastic basket. "Do you know what those are used for?" he asked.

"I think so," I said, nodding.

I heard Elizabeth giggle behind me from the bleachers.

"Good!" said Cowboy Bob. Then he pointed across the arena toward the horse stalls. "For safety's sake, I want you to start working in the empty stalls," he said. "Halley's back there now. Later, you can work in the arena. You can stay pretty busy around here just gathering apples."

"Apples?" I asked. I didn't see any apples.

Cowboy Bob winked at me. "Sounds better than *manure*, don't you think?" he asked. "Either way, it's what comes with horses. No way around it."

I wrinkled up my face.

"Are ya still willing to help out?" Cowboy Bob asked.

"Yup," I said, without hesitating. "Ready to work."

Cowboy Bob smiled and put his hand on my

shoulder. "Don't worry," he said. "This won't be the only job here for you. But everyone pitches in, and it's important to keep this place tidy—both for horses and for riders."

Cowboy Bob showed me around the stalls and where to empty the wheelbarrow when I was finished.

Cleaning up after horses is a big jump from cleaning up after hamsters, but honestly, I didn't mind it all that much. It felt good to do something useful. And the riding center definitely wouldn't be very pleasant if the work didn't get done.

I wheeled the barrow into the barn and went from one empty stall to another, scooping up "apples." When I passed the sliding door, I looked for Josie in the arena. There she was! I waved as Josie rode by. When she saw my wheelbarrow full of horse apples, she giggled and gave me a thumbs-up.

When the wheelbarrow was full—and heavy— I pushed it outside through a side door and emptied it onto a large mound. As I wheeled back in past the stalls, I noticed one horse tied up in the far stall. Halley was talking in the horse's ear.

I parked my wheelbarrow and walked closer. The horse stood in his stall, cross-tied—ropes clipped to each side of his halter—under a stall plate that read "Dusty." With a coat of dapple gray and soft, gentle eyes, he nickered at me as I approached. Then he bobbed his head up and down. Was he saying hello? I felt an instant bond with Dusty, as if we'd been friends a long time.

"Why isn't Dusty out in the arena?" I asked Halley.

"Oh, he's not ready," she explained. "He still needs work before he's spook-proof. Cowboy Bob's been working with him on that."

"Spook-proof?" someone asked from behind me. I jumped and whirled around. It was Josie, who was maneuvering her chair down the aisle between stalls.

"Sheesh, Josie!" I said, trying to catch my breath. *"You* spooked *me."*

"Sorry!" she said. "I got done with riding and wanted to see what you were doing back here. So what were you saying about 'spook-proof'?"

"Hi, Josie," Halley said warmly. "I was just telling McKenna that 'spook-proof' means a horse won't flinch at anything. We prefer to have only steady, confident horses here. But Dusty is a recent donation. We're still working with him."

I backed away.

"Oh, don't worry," Halley said. "He's sweet. You can pet him."

I reached out and stroked Dusty's velvety gray and pink muzzle. Josie scratched the underside of his neck, and he closed his eyes in contentment. "But how does Cowboy Bob make horses spook-proof?" I asked.

"Well, let's see if I can show you," said Halley. "Better step back."

I left Dusty and stepped a few feet down the aisle. Josie wheeled her chair backward to join me.

"First, I'll take off Dusty's cross-ties so that he doesn't feel trapped," said Halley, unclipping the ropes from Dusty's halter. Then she clipped on a lead rope and, with her other hand, slowly reached for a broomstick with a white plastic bag attached to its end.

"Lots of horses are scared to death of these bags," she said as she lifted the bag and slowly inched it through the air toward Dusty. His eyes widened until the whites showed. Then he started dancing backward, trying to get away from the bag.

Halley held the broomstick still until Dusty's stance relaxed a little. "That's a brave boy," she cooed. "He's scared of plastic bags, but Cowboy Bob and I will work with him over and over again until he realizes plastic bags won't hurt him. Eventually, he'll think they're as scary as a fly."

"Uh-huh," I said. "It's the same with gymnastics. Things I used to be terrified to try now seem easy to me."

"Me, too!" said Josie. "I mean, not with gymnastics, but with horseback riding. I can't believe I was ever afraid to ride sweet, gentle Pumpkin."

Halley smiled. "I hope Dusty will become spook-proof just as quickly as you girls have," she said, cross-tying Dusty again.

"I hope so, too," I murmured, giving Dusty a gentle kiss on the nose.

As Josie and I left the stables, I stopped by the bleachers so that I could say good-bye to Elizabeth. She was talking with a girl I didn't know, so I waited for a moment. I leaned against the bleachers and did a few calf-strengthening exercises, just as Willow had taught me. I rolled up on the balls of my feet—*hold, two, three*—and down again. I needed to use every free moment to rebuild strength.

"Hey, McKenna!"

I looked up and saw Elizabeth stepping down

the bleachers toward me.

"What are you doing?" she asked.

"Working out," I answered with a grin.

"You and Toulane," said Elizabeth, laughing good-naturedly. "You're two peas in a pod, y'know that? Working out is all she thinks about, too."

My smile faded, and I didn't answer. I guess I'd rather be compared with Sierra, who works hard but knows how to keep it fun at gymnastics. Or Josie, who gives her all at the riding center each week. But Toulane? I'd never felt more distant from her.

Mr. Wu strolled between our desks on Wednesday, smiling as if he'd just announced a class trip to SeaWorld. "A research project!" he said again. "It'll be great. I want you each to pick a partner to work with—quietly—and decide on a subject you can both get excited about."

"Partners?" Elizabeth whispered, leaning across the aisle toward my desk. With our new seating arrangement, Elizabeth now sat across from me and Toulane sat behind me.

At the same moment, I felt a tap-tap on my shoulder. I twisted around in my seat to face Toulane.

"Hey, let's be partners," she blurted. "We can research gymnastics."

"Oh, Elizabeth just asked me," I said. "Sorry."

Instantly I could see the hurt rise in Toulane's eyes.

"Um, maybe Mr. Wu will let us work as a group?" I said to Elizabeth.

But by the time I got the words out, Toulane had already left her desk and was heading across the room to find another partner. Her face wore the same steely expression that I'd seen so often lately. Somehow, I'd managed to mess things up with her—*again*.

Volunteer Day

Later that day, I met Josie in the library. I tried to work on my homework, but I was too bothered by Toulane's storminess to concentrate.

Halfway through an assignment, I lifted my head from my book and groaned.

"What?" Josie asked.

"I don't know what's *wrong* with her," I said.

Josie pulled lip gloss from her pocket. "Who?" she asked.

"Toulane," I said. "She's so hard to deal with lately."

Josie shrugged. "She's probably stressed out about making the competitive team," she said. "Same as you."

I felt a flutter of nerves in my stomach. "Don't remind me," I said. "Still, I wish she wouldn't take it out on me."

With her elbow on the arm of her wheelchair, Josie leaned her chin into her open palm. "Maybe she needs to think about something completely different," she said. "When I'm stressed, helping someone *else* takes my mind off *me*."

I cracked up. "Is that why you tutor me?"

I asked her. "To bring your stress down?"

Josie smiled. "That's part of it," she joked.

I hoped Toulane would decide to join our volunteer day at the riding center. She'd have a chance to help someone else and take her mind off her worries. If nothing else, it might take her mind off being crabby with *me*—at least for a few hours.

★

Finally the day came! Our level-four group drove together in the Shooting Star club van to Hearts and Horses.

Shannon met us at the door. "Welcome, girls!" she said warmly. Then she gave our group a tour of the center. When we stopped by the arena, Shannon paused by the fence. "McKenna, would you like to introduce some of our riders?" she asked.

"Sure," I agreed, glancing around the arena to make sure I knew most of the riders.

"Leaders!" Shannon called out. "Please swing by the meet-and-greet area so that our guests can meet today's riders."

Instead of stepping up toward the fence, some of my teammates shrank back. Toulane hovered a few feet behind me, her arms crossed.

Volunteer Day

I remembered feeling nervous, too, my first time at the riding center. I hoped I could find a way to help my teammates feel more relaxed.

When Dora rode toward us in her pink helmet, I said, "This is Dora, who rides with her teddy bear."

Sierra whispered, "Oh, she's adorable!" She waved at Dora, but as Dora rode closer and her lopsided face became more visible, Sierra looked away. When I'd first seen Dora close-up, I felt uncomfortable, too—and a little afraid and sad. Today, all I noticed was her cheery smile.

When Dora saw *my* face, her smile widened. She sat up straight and said, "Pur-ble in, in, in!"

"Wait, what did she say?" Sierra asked.

"Gray OUT!" Dora shouted as she rode past us.

Sierra's jaw dropped. "Did you teach her our gymnastics trick?" she asked, punching me playfully in the arm. Coach Isabelle caught my eye, too, and grinned.

I nodded, feeling pretty proud of myself—and of Dora.

Just then, wide-eyed Julius rode Oreo near our end of the arena. I waved as he passed.

"That's Julius—Elizabeth Onishi's brother," I said to Toulane, who was still standing behind me.

"Seriously? Her brother?" Toulane asked, taking a step forward.

"Yup," I said, turning back toward the arena.

When Josie rode by, I called out, "Hey, Josie! How's it going?"

"Great!" Josie called back. "Pumpkin is the best horse ever." She gripped the saddle horn with one hand and patted the horse's neck with the other.

Toulane nudged me from behind and said, "Hey, I thought Josie used a wheelchair."

"She does," I said. "And she's learning to ride, too."

Toulane didn't say anything else, but as Josie and Pumpkin did a full lap around the arena, Toulane's eyes followed them every step of the way.

⸺⭑

When the riding session was over, my teammates and I followed Shannon to the kitchen. A half-dozen young riders were waiting for us. I was glad to see that Josie was there, too.

To my surprise, Shannon asked, "Josie and McKenna, would you two help organize groups? You'll want to mix up your teammates with our riders so that everyone can get to know one another."

"Of course!" Josie said, jumping right in.

I was pleased, too. First, we asked everyone to count off by fours, which left us with four groups of four. When everyone was in groups, Josie and I thought up a get-to-know-you game. Josie suggested that the riders tell their names and the names of the horses they loved to ride.

Then I said, "And everyone from Shooting Star, tell what is your favorite gymnastics event—vault, bars, beam, or floor."

After introductions, Shannon explained our baking tasks for the afternoon. "We like to have treats on hand for our riders to offer to their horses as a thank-you after riding," she said.

"What about treats for people?" Josie piped up, grinning.

"And we'll make cookies for people," Shannon said with a smile. "Of course!"

Some of us mixed up cookie dough, while others mixed up horse-treat dough. We cracked eggs and measured flour, salt, oats, honey, and molasses. We made chocolate-chip cookies by dropping spoonfuls of dough onto baking sheets. And we rolled out horse-treat dough with rolling pins and cut out round treats with cookie cutters.

Sierra found a stepstool for her kitchenmate, a girl whose legs were too short for her to work at the counter. "Thank you!" the girl exclaimed.

Before long, the kitchen was filled with the delicious smells of cookies and molasses horse treats baking. We cooled and tasted the cookies as they came out of the oven, batch after batch.

All of my teammates seemed to be having fun, except Toulane. She had been assigned to work with Josie, Julius, and me. Instead, Toulane busied herself sweeping the floor and watching the cookies bake in the oven, her back turned toward our group.

Toulane was such a leader in the gym, but outside of gymnastics, she didn't seem nearly as sure of herself. Working with new people—and new and different situations—was one of Josie's strengths, but it sure didn't seem to be one of Toulane's.

Josie must have noticed, too. "Hey, Toulane," she called in a friendly voice. "Want to help us mix up another batch of horse treats?"

I looked up from rolling out dough, grateful that Josie was trying to help Toulane feel comfortable. But I wondered what Toulane would do.

To my relief, she nodded and turned back around to face our group.

Julius held a wooden spoon in his hand. He
held it out toward Toulane and mumbled, "Me Julius."

Toulane shrank back, her brow wrinkled.
"What?" she said. "I can't understand him."

"He says his name is Julius," Josie said gently.

I couldn't blame Toulane for shrinking away.
My first time at the riding center, all I saw were the
riders' disabilities—the ways they were different from
me. But now I was learning to see all the ways we were
the same. Julius's smile told me that he was having
just as much fun making cookies and meeting friends
as I was. I wished Toulane could see what I saw.

"Come on, Toulane," I said, reaching for her
hand. "We need your help measuring."

Toulane shook her head. She stepped away and
motioned for me to follow her. Then she whispered,
"I'm just not good at this. At being here."

"I know how you feel," I said, shrugging.
"The first time I came here, I felt the same way. It
takes time, that's all."

"What if I say or do something wrong?"
Toulane whispered back, her eyes wide with worry.

I wished Josie could answer Toulane's question.
She'd know what to say. I was afraid I would blow it.
Then I thought about all the times Toulane and I had

faced something new together at the gym.

"Toulane," I said quietly, "you know when you're about to try a new gymnastics move? You're nervous, aren't you?"

Toulane narrowed her eyes at me, but then nodded.

I whispered, "So how do you get through that?"

Toulane thought about it for a moment. "I'd take a few deep breaths," she finally said. "Blue sky in . . . or maybe purple." She gave me a half-smile.

I giggled. "So can you shake off your stress here in the same way?" I asked.

A glimmer of understanding crossed Toulane's face. "Maybe," she said quietly. She drew in a deep breath slowly, and then exhaled slowly. She nodded, and I knew she was ready to try.

"You'll do fine," I assured her.

Toulane raised her chin, pressed back her shoulders, and stepped closer to Julius. "Hi, Julius," she said, sounding much more friendly and confident. "I'm Toulane. Um, want to work together?"

"I working hard!" he said and began wildly stirring the wooden spoon around and around in the empty bowl. *Clankety, clank, clank!*

Volunteer Day

"Want to help measure flour?" Toulane asked.

"I helping!" Julius said, but he kept stirring.

Toulane cleared her throat. "Okay. Um, I'll measure flour," she said. "You, um, just keep stirring." She measured flour and added it to the bowl.

"I good at stirring," he said.

"Yes, you're very good," Toulane agreed, forcing a quick smile. "Now, I'll crack a few eggs. I'll add those and you can stir."

When Toulane glanced at me over Julius's curly head, I gave her a thumbs-up. I admired her for reaching out to Julius, despite feeling uncomfortable.

I turned back to rolling out dough. Nearby, Sierra was singing as she worked with her group. For just a moment, all was right with the world.

Crack! I turned. Julius must have stirred a little too hard, because he was staring at his wooden spoon, now on the floor. His lower lip protruded. He looked at the spoon, and then he starting crying.

I waited a second to see if Toulane would help Julius, but she looked bewildered by his tears. She inched backward toward Coach Isabelle. I hustled over, picked up the spoon, and showed it to Julius.

"I good stirrer," he said, a fleck of butter dangling from a dark curl. He reached for the spoon.

"Yes," I said, patting his shoulder. "But I need to wash this first—or get a new one," I told him.

Julius cried harder. "Not new one!" he insisted.

I hurried over to the sink and washed the spoon. I dried it quickly with a towel and handed it back to Julius. "Here you go!" I said cheerfully.

His lower lip trembled.

"You're a good stirrer, Julius," I said. "Want to try again?"

Julius sniffled, nodded, and returned to stirring. He started humming, and before long he said, "I happy-happy."

I looked around for Toulane, but she was gone.

When the lunch bell rang on Monday,
Toulane was the first of my classmates out the door.
She had been avoiding me all morning, ever since
things hadn't worked out for her at the riding center.

As I headed for the door, Mr. Wu stopped me.
"McKenna, I need a word with you," he said.

Uh-oh. Had he noticed that something was
wrong between me and Toulane? Or was I in trouble
again with schoolwork? A streak of panic swept
through me like hot lava, but I reminded myself that
my grades were up. All my homework was in on time.

"McKenna," Mr. Wu said, as the last student
left the room, "you've made such great progress in
reading and schoolwork that as far as I'm concerned,
you don't have to meet with a tutor anymore." He
beamed at me. "Great work!"

I didn't know what to say. I was thrilled to hear
that I'd made progress and that my teacher was no
longer worried about me. I should have felt happy and
proud.

Instead, I felt sad and a little worried, too, about
not meeting with Josie anymore. Having her help was
like having a spotter at the gym to catch me if I fell.
What if I fell behind again in schoolwork? What if
I never saw Josie again? I stared at the door handle.

I must have worn my mixed feelings on my face, because Mr. Wu said, "That is, unless you don't *want* to stop working with Josie." He paused and said, "McKenna, it's entirely up to you."

I looked up at Mr. Wu and asked, "Can I meet with her at least one more time?"

"Of course," he agreed.

As I stepped into the hallway's flow of students, another wave of worry washed over me. I wasn't ready to stop meeting with Josie yet. Would I ever be?

On Wednesday, I left class early and headed to the school library. As I walked down the hall, my feet felt heavy. The first few sessions with Josie, I had dragged my feet because I didn't want to be tutored. Now, I hated to think our meetings were coming to an end. With a twinge, I pushed through the swinging double doors.

I'd come to love meeting within the library's walls, surrounded by the smell of countless books and the soft voices of students and teachers. I headed toward our usual table, where Josie was already parked. She smiled, but her dimples weren't quite as deep as usual.

No More Tutor?

"Hey, congratulations!" Josie said. "My teacher said your grades are up and you don't need tutoring anymore."

"Thanks," I said quietly, setting my backpack on the table. "Josie, I should be happy about that . . . but what if I start falling behind again?"

Josie laughed lightly, but her eyes looked a little sad, too. "You'll do fine, McKenna," she said. "But we can still get together whenever you want to."

"You mean if I'm stuck?" I asked.

"Sure," she said. "Or not stuck. I may not be your tutor, but we can always be friends."

"Oh," I said, letting out a deep breath. "That makes me feel better."

Working with Josie had become more than just tutoring. I'd hoped to make progress with schoolwork, but I'd never imagined we'd become friends. Now, in so many ways, I felt Josie knew and understood me better than anyone.

Josie smiled and said, "If you start struggling with schoolwork, I'm just a phone call, text, or visit away. Got it?"

"Got it!" I said. And then, instead of worry, I felt a surge of *everything's-going-to-be-fine* feeling.

Being half-funny and half-serious, I held an

imaginary phone to my ear, thumb up and pinky toward my mouth. "Hello?" I said. "Is Josie there?"

Josie played along and picked up her imaginary phone. "May I help you?" she answered.

"I have a problem," I said.

"Yes?" Josie said officially. "Well, jump right in—what's bothering you?"

Then I put my hand on the table, and Josie did, too. I looked her in the eyes. She'd been so helpful in so many ways. Maybe she could help me with this bigger problem, too.

"I tried to help Toulane feel better about being at the riding center, but now she won't talk to me," I said.

"Hmm," said Josie, tilting her head. "Yeah, she didn't look very happy on Volunteer Day."

I leaned into my open palms. "She seems so uncomfortable with my friendship with you, with the riding center—with all of it," I said.

"You mean," Josie whispered, "uncomfortable with people with disabilities?"

I nodded. "I guess I just wish the riding center could help Toulane the way it helps me," I said. "I feel better by volunteering there. It helps me take my mind off making the team in March."

"I know," Josie said with a nod. "For me, the riding center helps me relax and forget about some of my other challenges for a while. My mom calls it 'the B word.'"

"Huh?" I asked. "What's that?"

"Balance," said Josie as she reached up and turned her earring between her fingers.

I thought of Toulane and how she must be feeling extra pressure to succeed at the gym, now that her sister couldn't compete. Her mom was focused on Toulane's every move. "That's what Toulane needs," I agreed. "A little more balance."

I flashed back to how good Toulane had been with Julius when she first started mixing cookie dough with him—*before* the spoon incident. Maybe the riding center could still work for her. Maybe she just needed more good experiences like that to help her feel more comfortable. "What if I invited her back to Hearts and Horses sometime?" I asked.

Josie shrugged. "Think she'd say yes?" she asked.

"I don't know. Probably not," I said. "But I can always ask, right?"

Josie picked up her imaginary phone again and said, "Right."

✦

That night over a lasagna dinner—with
Cooper under the table, hoping for someone to drop
a slice of garlic bread—I told Mom and Dad that I'd
"graduated" from needing a tutor.

"Bravo, McKenna!" said Mom, lifting her glass.
We all toasted with glasses of milk.

After dinner, while Mom read to the twins,
Dad and I worked on dishes. With his hands in sink
water, Dad asked, "Where should we go?"

"Go?" I said, not sure what he meant.

"To celebrate your hard work and graduation
from tutoring," said Dad.

"Oh. The top of the Space Needle?" I suggested, expecting to hear the same old answer: "It's
too expensive." The Needle towers above the harbor
in downtown Seattle, and from the top, you can see
the whole city. Just below the rooftop is the revolving
SkyCity Restaurant, which I'd never been to before.
I didn't hold my breath.

Dad gave me a wink.

"Really?" I asked.

He nodded and went back to scrubbing a
skillet. "What you've accomplished is huge, and so

important," he said. "When you learned you were falling behind, you could have just shrugged your shoulders and said 'so what?'—and fallen further behind."

My cheeks burned with happiness. It felt so good to know Dad was proud of me.

He kept talking and scrubbing. "I see lots of kids like that at the high school," he said. "They slip behind somewhere early on and never catch up. So, yes, I *want* to do something extra special—our own awards celebration. You've worked hard at school *and* at gymnastics. That's no easy feat!" He hugged me with one arm, keeping his dripping wet hand outstretched over the sink.

"At the top of the Space Needle?" I said excitedly. "Really? When? I can't wait!"

"Well," Dad said, "we'll have to work on that. I have so many meetings lately I can barely see straight. But we'll schedule it just as soon as we can. And, McKenna, would you like to invite a friend?"

I instantly thought about both Josie and Sierra. I wouldn't be where I was in school or at the gym without their support. But then I thought of Toulane. Even if things felt broken between us now, she'd been there for me for years. Maybe inviting her could be a good way to patch things up.

"Dad?" I asked as I wiped dishes. "I have an extra special request. Could, um, Josie and Toulane *both* come?"

Dad paused to think about it. "If that's what you would like," he finally said, "then that's what you'll get."

"Thanks, Dad!" I said, hugging his waist. I felt like dancing and leaping across the kitchen. Instead, I spun around, planted my feet, and stretched out my arms in a gymnastics salute.

Dad turned sideways and started clapping, sending water droplets across the floor—and me.

I cracked up and took a bow.

★

That night, I wrote a note to Toulane. I really couldn't give up on our friendship. We always sat near each other in class and worked out three times a week at the gym together. Our friendship was worth fighting for.

It was hard to know what to say in my note. It took me a few drafts to get the words just right, but finally it read:

Hi, Toulane,

I know things have been hard between us lately, but I want our friendship to work. Can we start over and try again?

My parents are taking me to dinner at the top of the Needle sometime soon, and I want you and Josie to come, too. Will you? Hope you say yes!

McKenna

The next day in class, I passed the note over my shoulder and dropped it onto Toulane's desk.

I heard her unfold the note, and I held my breath, waiting for her reaction. I wondered if she'd say something mean, or worse yet, say nothing at all. But as I stole a backward glance, I saw a half-smile on Toulane's lips.

A few minutes later, I heard Toulane tear a sheet of paper from her notebook and scribble something on it. She tapped the back of my shoe with her toe, her signal that a note was coming my way.

I reached down to pick up the note from the floor—carefully, because Mr. Wu was at the board doing math problems—and opened it. Her note said: *Really? My answer is YES!!!*

We exchanged smiles.

Before class ended, I wrote another note and handed it to Toulane. It said:

Hi again.
I'm so glad you said YES!
And I'm sorry things didn't work out at the riding center. You were really GOOD at helping Julius before he dropped his spoon, and I liked having you there. Will you give the center one more try—for me?

I didn't hear back from Toulane until the end of the day, when she was leaving to catch her bus. She pressed a new note into my palm, and I read it right away. It said: *I'll check with my mom.*

Chapter 8

Searching for Balance

At school on Friday, Toulane said she'd "try" to show up at Hearts and Horses. But that afternoon at the riding center, I wondered if she really would.

I waited on the bleachers alone, wondering where Elizabeth was today. She and her brother must have had something else going on.

As I watched Josie riding, I noticed a freestanding basketball hoop set up at the far end of the arena. One of the riders tossed a basketball toward the hoop when he rode past. When he missed, a volunteer retrieved the ball for him, and he tried again.

"Hey, McKenna," Shannon said, pausing by the bleachers. "Josie's lucky to have such a good friend coaching her."

"Me?" I laughed, pointing to my chest. "I don't know *anything* about riding—just gymnastics."

Shannon thought for a minute. Then she said, "I know you've learned things in gymnastics that already help here, too."

I instantly thought of Dora, breathing in purple and breathing out gray, and I nodded. I guess gymnastics and horseback riding aren't that different after all.

Just then, to my surprise, Toulane walked into the arena. I jumped up to greet her. "Shannon, this is

Toulane," I said, waving to my friend. "She's a gymnast, too."

"Really? Great!" Shannon said. "I just might ask for some tips from you two, okay?"

I couldn't imagine how else we might help, but I nodded.

Toulane wore an *I'm-not-sure-I-want-to-be-here* expression, but I ignored it. She'd shown up. That was a start.

"Hey, let's get some popcorn and come back and watch the riders," I suggested.

Toulane followed me back out to the lobby, where the old-fashioned red popcorn machine was busily popping. *Pop-pop-pop-pop-pop!* Golden popcorn rose inside the glass walls. I grabbed two paper serving bags and filled them from the dispenser. Then we headed back into the arena and munched and talked while we watched from the bleachers.

"Look, Josie's riding better, isn't she?" I said as Josie passed by, reins in hand. She waved at us.

Toulane leaned forward, her elbows on her knees. "Yeah, she's actually pretty good," she admitted.

"There's a lot that Josie does well," I added, "and things she's still working on."

"Like what?" Toulane asked.

"Like facing her fear of falling," I replied.

Toulane fell silent. I glanced at her and noticed that she had hardly touched her popcorn. Her fingernails were chewed so short that the skin at the edges looked pink and raw.

"Maybe we're the same that way—you, me, and Josie," I said gently. "We all get scared sometimes."

Toulane turned toward me, her brown eyes intense and serious, and said, "McKenna, I'm so scared that I won't make the competitive team. My mom reminds me almost every day that tryouts are coming and that I have to do my best. I can barely breathe just thinking about it all."

She looked so miserable. Why couldn't gymnastics be fun for her anymore?

"Toulane, you're good, you really are," I said. "But I don't want to see you feeling this bad. It seems like you haven't had any fun in a long, long time."

She didn't answer, but I could tell she was listening, so I dove in and said what I'd been wanting to say.

I tilted my head. "Coming to the riding center has helped me, weirdly, to feel less stressed about everything—to be more *balanced*, you know?" I said.

Toulane nodded and then began working on

82

the edge of a fingernail.

As I looked out into the arena, wondering what to say next, Shannon caught my eye. She waved us over to the edge of the arena.

"Girls," she called up to us, "some of our riders could use help with balance. Have a few tips you could share with them?"

Toulane and I glanced at each other, mouths wide open.

"*Balance?*" I whispered to Toulane, my head close to hers. "There's that word again."

Toulane giggled but then got all serious and whispered back, "I don't have any tips to share. I'm not a rider!"

"Me neither," I said. "But we're gymnasts. Remember the first time we stepped onto the balance beam? We fell off, and it was the *low* beam!"

Toulane laughed. "We were *terrible* back then," she said, shaking her head.

"Yeah," I said. "We had to *learn* how to balance. Should we try this, too?"

A playful spark lit up Toulane's eyes. "Okay," she said. "We can try."

As Toulane and I stepped down the bleachers toward the fence, Shannon signaled a young rider

toward the edge of the arena. It was Julius! He rode
over on Oreo with the help of a leader and two side-
walkers.

"Hey there, Julius!" I said.

Curls of hair escaped his zebra helmet. I waited
for him to answer, but his eyes were fixed only on
Toulane. "Me 'member you!"

"You do?" said Toulane, looking more pleased
than uncomfortable this time. I was glad things were
starting out well.

Shannon said, "Julius has a way of leaning too
far forward in the saddle. Any ideas for him, girls?"

Toulane crossed her arms tightly. Was she
going to freeze up again?

"Julius," I said, "think of yourself as a puppet."

He closed his mouth into a tight line. Maybe he
thought that acting like a puppet meant he couldn't
speak or something.

Toulane smiled. "Julius?" she said. "Imagine
you have a string attached to the top of your head."

Julius lifted his eyebrows high, eyes widening.

With a little laugh, Toulane stepped up closer
to Julius and faced him. "Imagine that the string is
holding you up," she said. "Now what if someone
pulled that string up a little higher . . ." Toulane

pretended to lift a string higher above her own head, and as she did, her eyebrows rose and she stood up a little taller.

Julius put his hand on top of his helmet and patted it. Then he mirrored Toulane's example and pulled with a clenched fist upward—more like pulling on a heavy rope than on a string, but it worked, because Julius sat up taller by an inch or two.

"And a little higher still . . ." Toulane said, rising to her tiptoes. "Great! That's really good! Now, take a deep breath." Again, she demonstrated. "Let your shoulders drop as you let your breath out. But stay tall! You're still a puppet on a string!"

"Okay, Julius," Shannon said. "Can you try that while you ride?" Julius nodded and set off again, this time sitting taller and straighter in the saddle.

I nudged Toulane. "Look at him!" I said.

"Wow," Toulane whispered, wearing a pleased expression.

When Josie rode up next on Pumpkin, she looked more relaxed than I'd seen her yet at the center. "Hi, Josie," Shannon said. "We're working on some great tips for balance and posture, but you're looking at ease on your horse—like a real pro!"

Toulane piped up and said, "You *are* a good

rider. I don't have a clue how to do that."

"I'm just a beginner," Josie said, flushing a little, "but every week I learn something new about horses. Like a horse's ears. Watch where Pumpkin's ears turn, and you can see what she's paying attention to."

"Pumpkin," Toulane said, "I'm talking to you—are you listening?"

Pumpkin's right ear pivoted toward Toulane.

Toulane smiled. "Cool!" she said.

Josie waved and started riding again, joining the line right behind Julius. He was still sitting tall, like a proud little puppet.

After about half an hour, Julius and the other young riders began dismounting while some older, more experienced riders entered the arena. I saw Cowboy Bob lead Dusty into the arena, too. He was walking the horse without a saddle, probably to get him used to being around a few other horses and riders. Josie was still on her horse, riding just behind Logan—the teenage boy who was such an amazing rider, even though he couldn't see.

Suddenly, something caught my eye from across the arena. A side door swung open, and in blew a tumbling page of newspaper.

Dusty, his eyes showing white, started

prancing sideways, but Cowboy Bob held the rope.

"Oh no," I said under my breath.

The sheet of newspaper lifted on the air and touched down, then lifted again, as if it were a ghost chasing after Dusty. The horse tossed his head, reared, and bolted, all in a flash. Not even Cowboy Bob could hold on to him!

As Dusty raced around the arena, Shannon stepped up to the platform and took charge. "Halley," she said in a loud but calm voice, "try to help Bob with Dusty."

Halley walked slowly toward Dusty, but he turned and ran again, back past Pumpkin and Josie. Pumpkin jumped sideways, spooking, too. Josie leaned forward, clutching the saddle desperately.

Hang on, Josie! I willed her, gripping the fence railing in my hands.

The newspaper billowed again and blew toward my edge of the arena. Shannon's eyes were on the paper, too. "McKenna," she called to me, "can you reach it?"

I didn't waste a second. I knelt down and reached below the fence. I grabbed the newspaper and squashed it down into a ball in my hands.

Dusty stopped in place. His nostrils flared

and his flanks heaved, but that crazy-scared look was gone from his eyes. I felt as if I'd just performed a magic trick!

When I looked back at Josie, she was no longer riding Pumpkin. She was lying in a heap on the sand with Britta kneeling beside her.

Toulane and I gasped at the same time. I raced toward the gate, but by the time I got there, Shannon and Josie's mom were already helping Josie sit up, and she was smiling.

Shannon glanced toward me. "McKenna and Toulane, can you please bring Josie's wheelchair here?"

I was happy to have something to do, and by the look of relief on Toulane's face, I could tell she was, too. She pushed the wheelchair while I opened the gate.

"Josie!" I exclaimed as we got closer. "Are you okay?"

"I'm fine," Josie said sheepishly. "It was an adventure!"

"You're so brave," Toulane said. "Can I borrow some of that courage for team tryouts?"

"All you want," Josie said with a grin.

Shannon and Josie's mom helped Josie into

her wheelchair, and Josie let me wheel her out of the arena. Before we left, Cowboy Bob stopped me. "Hey, cowgirl, good thinking back there," he said, placing his hand on my shoulder.

"Thanks," I said.

He lifted his cowboy hat and rubbed his forehead. "I sure thought we had Dusty spook-proofed," he said, "but we hadn't tested him around newspaper. Looks like we have some more work to do."

While Toulane and I waited for Josie to turn in her helmet and check out, Toulane said, "That was pretty exciting."

I still felt a little shaky about it all. "Yeah, I'm so glad Josie didn't get hurt," I said.

"Me, too," Toulane agreed. And I could tell by the tone of her voice that she really meant it.

Two weeks flew by, and I worked extra hard at the gym, building strength—and confidence. Team tryouts were now only nine days away, and the tension was skyrocketing. Toulane, Sierra, and I were more focused than ever, and Coach Isabelle was, too. On Thursday afternoon, she pulled us aside.

"Girls," she said, "I've always emphasized fun, but from now until March-fest, I want you to take every bit of energy you have—mental and physical— and really push yourselves. There will be girls from other gyms competing for spots on the team. I'd love to see each of you move up to the competitive team, but only you and your performance can determine the results."

Standing beside Toulane, I saw the muscles clench in her jaw. Like an old-fashioned clock, she was winding up tighter and tighter, to the point where I thought she might break. But at least she wasn't taking her stress out on me. Ever since our last time at the riding center, things had been easier between us.

Coach Isabelle whispered, "I believe in you girls. Now believe in yourselves, too! Let's go!"

Then we set off to perform our routines, cheering one another on.

When the compulsory music started, I began,

determined this time to do the round-off back hand-spring without Coach Isabelle's help. If I needed help at tryouts, I'd get a deduction, and my score would be lower. But if I could do the move successfully on my own, I'd get extra points. All I had to do was keep my upper arms extended as I completed the element.

My ankle was getting stronger with each practice, but I still felt it and thought about it with every move. Halfway through my routine, I pivoted in the corner and headed across the mat, where Coach Isabelle waited for me—just in case. I stretched my body into the round-off, but as I attempted the back handspring, my arms bent again. I crashed down, squashing my face against the mat.

"Ummpph!" I scrambled to my feet to finish my routine.

Coach Isabelle stood nearby. She must have figured I was okay, which I was—just so, *so* frustrated. I tried again. When the music stopped, I was still finishing. I struck a pose and then saluted—arms up.

Next up was Toulane. She performed her floor routine brilliantly! But instead of joining us afterward, she bolted—just like Dusty had at the arena—straight toward the bathroom.

After another teammate finished her routine,

Coach Isabelle said, "McKenna, will you please check the bathroom and see if Toulane is okay?"

With a nod I dashed across the gym and around other groups of gymnasts. I slowed to a walk as I passed the lockers and headed into the restroom. "Toulane?" I called, expecting her to be in a bathroom stall. But to my surprise, she was sitting on the tile floor under the hand-dryer. She was clutching her knees to her chest like a frightened little kid.

I dropped down beside her. "Oh, Toulane! What's wrong?" I asked, searching her face. "Do you have the flu?"

She shook her head. Her face was pale as egg-shells, her eyes red from crying.

My heart leapt out of my chest. "You're really stressed, aren't you?" I asked, touching her shoulder.

Toulane nodded. Then, gulping air, she sobbed, "I'm so . . . so stressed that I'm . . . I got sick to my stomach."

"Oh!" I said, jumping up to grab a paper towel. I wet it under the faucet. "Here, try this on your face," I said.

"Thanks," she said. She sniffled and pressed the damp towel against her face. "I don't know what happened out there," she said, her voice muffled.

"I was doing fine until I started thinking about team tryouts, and then I just . . . freaked out."

I sat against the wall beside her, shoulder to shoulder. "You know how Dusty freaked out about that newspaper?" I asked.

Toulane nodded, her chin trembling.

"We all freak out sometimes," I said. "I mean, nobody is *completely* spook-proof, right?"

Toulane's shoulders shuddered with a jagged breath. "I just feel like I have to be a big success for my mom," she said. "I'm scared I'm going to let her down. What if I freeze up next week right in the middle of a routine?"

I didn't say that if anyone should be afraid, it should be me. After all, I was the one overcoming an injury. I was scared that my ankle might give out and that I'd fall—and maybe even hurt myself all over again.

"You could freeze up," I said. "I could, too. But I don't think we will. We've practiced so much, over and over . . . "

Toulane nodded her head and blew her nose. "The thing is, McKenna, I'm not even sure I *want* to be on the competitive team anymore," she said.

My stomach dropped. "What?" I said,

93

wondering if I'd heard her right. "Are you serious?"

"Well, if I could choose," Toulane said, staring at the bright lights above the sink, "I'd do rhythmic gymnastics instead."

I caught my breath. "You would?" I asked. "But I thought—"

Toulane waved off my concern. "Don't worry, McKenna," she said. "My mom would kill me if I changed sports."

I was speechless. I'd always assumed Toulane wanted to do artistic gymnastics more than anything in the world. But maybe I'd been wrong. The thought of not practicing with Toulane at the gym left me feeling shaky. No wonder she'd struggled when she thought I was pulling away.

I wanted Toulane on the competitive team, but if she wasn't happy . . . As her friend, I wanted to support her. I said, "Maybe you need to tell your mom how you feel."

Toulane shook her head. "No way. I told you, I can't change sports now." She started to stand up.

I reached up to grab her hand. I couldn't let her step back into the gym looking so sad. "Whatever you do, I'll support you," I said softly.

For just a moment, I thought Toulane might

start crying again, but instead, she smiled. "Thanks, McKenna," she said, her eyes still red. "You're a good friend."

Then I thought of a way to cheer her up. "Repeat after me," I said. "Purple in, in, in."

Toulane chuckled. Then she repeated, "Purple in, in, in," and inhaled deeply. I did the same.

"And?" I asked teasingly, holding my breath.

We exhaled hard and exclaimed, "Gray OUT!"

I stood up and we hugged—long and strong— and, together, returned to the gym.

★

On Saturday, after working out hard at the gym, I was happy to go and help at Hearts and Horses. It was the center's open house and a chance for people to come and see what the center was all about. It gave the riders a chance to show off their new skills, and it gave *me* a chance to think about something other than gymnastics for a few hours. Team tryouts were now only one week away, and my mind kept running over every detail of my routines.

I'd invited Toulane and Sierra to join me at the open house, so after practice, Grandma Peg drove us to the riding center and dropped us off.

After grabbing a few bags of popcorn, we met up in the arena with Josie, her purple helmet in her lap. She pointed to a rider at the far end of the arena. "You've gotta watch," Josie said. "That's Devin—she's fifteen—riding English."

On a tall, prancing black horse, a teenager rode in a saddle without a saddle horn and with thin steel stirrups. She rode her horse in circles at a walk and then a trot, and then she cantered the horse gracefully around the outer edge of the arena.

"She's really good!" Sierra said.

I agreed. If Devin had a disability, I didn't see it. All I saw was a skilled horse and rider.

Toulane leaned forward, mesmerized, and said, "Sometimes I forget that there are other sports besides gymnastics."

After several minutes, I glanced at the clock. "We'd better head to the kitchen," I said. "Visitors will be coming soon."

In the center's kitchen, we helped by making huge coolers of punch, taste-testing a few cookies, and setting out napkins and plates. When we finished, we searched for Shannon and found her on the mounting platform in the arena. "What can we do now to help?" Josie asked.

"I love that question," Shannon said, smiling. "I was hoping a couple of you could stay up here on the mounting platform to explain the wall chart to visitors. Would you mind?"

"Not a bit," Josie said.

"I'll help you," offered Toulane. Josie nodded and gave her a warm smile.

When Shannon asked if I could help fill popcorn bags, I happily agreed. As we walked out of the arena, Shannon said, "McKenna, I'm so impressed with how you've helped some of the riders with balance and breathing. You're really good with them."

"Thanks," I said. "It's been fun."

"So, I'm wondering, would you consider volunteering here a few hours a week to keep working with some of our riders on balance and to help out in other ways, as needed?"

I hesitated. I wanted to spend more time at the center—I really did—but if I made the competitive gymnastics team, I wasn't sure I would have any free time left over. "I can't say for sure," I said to Shannon, "but I want to. Can I think about it and let you know?"

"Of course," Shannon said. "Keep me posted, alright?"

I nodded.

As I filled paper bags with warm popcorn, my head spun with the smell of salted butter and thoughts of everything that had been happening lately. Team tryouts were only seven days away! Questions popped through my mind like corn kernels exploding.

Would my ankle hold up during tryouts? Would I make the competitive team? If I did, would Toulane be there with me—and did she still want to be? Would I still have time to come back to the center with Josie? And even more time to volunteer with young riders? I just didn't know. *Pop, pop, pop, pop, pop . . .*

Chapter 10

A Basket of Butterflies

Something changed Thursday at the gym.

I stood at the edge of the mat, ankle taped, ready to try my round-off back handspring—again. Coach Isabelle was kneeling, ready to spot me. But it dawned on me that I had been so focused on my weakened ankle that I'd forgotten about the rest of my body. The handspring required my *arms* to be strong, too. And they *were*, after months of push-ups and rope climbing during practice.

I closed my eyes and visualized my arms holding the weight of my body off the mat. I saw myself completing the element perfectly—no wiping out or "kissing the mat" this time. I not only pictured the move, I *believed* I could do it.

Then I opened my eyes, gathered speed, and threw my body—smooth and strong—into the round-off back handspring. This time, without help, I landed it!

Coach Isabelle held out her hands toward me. We low-fived, and I couldn't stop smiling. Then I practiced over and over, until my body memorized the move.

The night before March-fest and team tryouts,

I went to bed at nine o'clock, but I didn't fall asleep until after eleven. And then, as if a rooster were crowing in my head, I woke up at three, four, and five. I fell back asleep for what seemed like only a second before Mom nudged me to get up at seven-thirty.

My stomach turned like a bolt—tighter and tighter—but I made myself eat scrambled eggs, sausage, and toast, knowing that I'd need energy.

Before heading off with my family, I taped and re-taped my ankle, making sure the tape was tight enough but not *too* tight. Then I pulled my warm-ups on over my leotard and hurried out to Grandma's Jeep.

The parking lot at Shooting Star Gymnastics was packed with cars. As we walked into the gym, I was overwhelmed by the noise and the rainbow of colors of different teams in their matching warm-ups and leotards. At the far side of the gym, Shooting Star's competitive team clustered around Coach Chip. I felt a little dizzy.

I spotted my family in the front row of the viewing area. Josie was parked beside them, at the end of the row of chairs. They all waved, and I forced a smile and waved back.

Breathe, I reminded myself as I felt my

shoulders rising and tensing.

Girls hovered near tables by the entry door selling March-fest sweatshirts, T-shirts, and caps. There were leotards for sale, plus posters of famous gymnasts, and lots of hair accessories.

"Look, candy!" Maisey exclaimed, pointing toward a table.

"Those are 'Candy Congrats,'" I explained. Candy Congrats were blank notes attached to candy. Families who bought the candy could write notes that would be read to gymnasts over the loudspeaker during the competition.

My family took turns wishing me well and kissing my cheek. And then they went to find seats.

I spotted Toulane and Sierra by the lockers. We were the only ones from our level-four group trying out for the competitive team, but girls from other clubs were trying out, too. Coach Isabelle said there would be seven girls competing for two spots. *Yikes.*

If I didn't make the team, I hoped the spots would go to Toulane and Sierra. But I had no idea how good the girls from the other clubs might be.

I stood beside my locker and pulled off my warm-up jacket. Then, as a surprise, I pulled from my backpack three matching braided bands of pink, orange, and yellow. "Friendship bracelets," I said, handing them to Toulane and Sierra.

"Oh, McKenna," Sierra said, her eyes bright.

"I gave one to Josie, too," I said. "She's here to cheer us on!"

"Cool," Toulane said, studying her bracelet and then meeting my eyes with a smile. "I wish we could wear them right now, but we'll have to wait till after we compete."

"That's right," Coach Isabelle said, joining us. And then she reminded us of what to expect of the tryouts. "You're competing against each other today, but you're still teammates. You need to encourage each other and help each other have fun!"

Her last word must have stuck, because Sierra, Toulane, and I broke into smiles as we set off after her. Heads high and shoulders back, we strode past the viewing area, packed with spectators. *No matter how I perform,* I reminded myself, *I'm happy to have family and friends who support me.* Plus, I was proud to be here after my ankle injury. I'd worked hard to heal and catch up.

A basket of butterflies trembled inside me.

All the gymnastics teams spread out on the mats to stretch for a half hour. Off to the side, I led my teammates in front splits while someone read Candy

Congrats over the loudspeakers.

"For McKenna Brooks," I suddenly heard. "You're our shooting star. We love you! Your family."

I smiled and waved at Mom, Dad, my grandparents, and my sisters. Then I turned back to face Toulane and Sierra. There was a definite hum of energy—coming not just from me, but from them, too. We were ready!

All too soon, warm-up time was over. Coach Chip stepped up to a microphone. Beside him was a pyramid of platforms numbered one through seven—the winners' podium. On either side of it, tall vases bloomed with bouquets of balloons and glittery stars.

"Welcome, welcome," Coach Chip began, as the gym quieted. "Welcome to March-fest, held this year at Shooting Star Gymnastics! Today clubs from the northwest region will be competing. In addition, we'll be holding open tryouts for Shooting Star's level-four competitive team. By the end of the day, two girls will be joining our team. They'll be back to compete next year!"

A round of applause went up from the first row of the audience. No one cheered louder than Toulane's mom and her sister, Tasha. I glanced at Toulane, wondering how she was holding up. She was looking at me—not at the crowd—and she gave me a thumbs-up, which I figured was a good sign.

"Go, Sierra!" I heard.

Mrs. Myers shouted, "McKenna! It's yours, girl!"

Mara and Maisey simply screamed my name, "McKenna!!!"

As teams marched in, Coach Chip introduced them. The cheers from the crowd were earsplitting.

I used to think that meets focused on only one gymnast at a time, but that's not how it works. It's like a big carnival, with every piece of equipment being used at once. And in level four, when girls do their floor routines, the same compulsory music starts up over and over again. When I heard the music begin for one of the competitive gymnasts, my heart raced.

Coach Isabelle signaled to Toulane, Sierra, and me to join her in one corner of the gym, along with four girls I didn't know.

"You'll be trying out on this side of the gym," she said. "I'll be taking notes, along with two visiting coaches."

And then it was time.

As instructed by Coach Isabelle, we lined up, ready for vault. I was last in line. Being last is both good and bad—bad because I had to wait and keep my butterflies under control, but good because I could cheer on Sierra and Toulane and watch their routines. That helped me focus on mine, too.

When it was my turn, I took a deep breath and visualized myself completing the move. Then I ran to the vault and sprang from my arms, landing flat-back on the blue elevated mats, solidly within the yellow boundary mark. *Yes!*

It all spun by—and our order kept rotating.

Uneven bars. I gained good momentum with my front hip circle.

Balance beam. I tottered once and nearly fell off, but I managed to regain my footing.

Floor exercise.

On floor, the routine I was most worried about, I was up first. Being first is good and bad—bad because I didn't have time to think, but good for the same reason.

I stepped up to the corner of the floor mat and tried to smile while I waited for a judge to signal me to start. When the man with the silver glasses lifted his hand, I saluted—arms extended upward.

And then, to my horror, I froze up!

Spooked.

My pulse pounded so loudly in my head that

I wasn't sure I'd hear the music when it started. My heart sped up like a racehorse, but my mind moved like a stubborn ox. I couldn't remember how to begin. I couldn't remember anything!

Time stood still, as if I were in a horrible dream.

Desperate, I glanced over at Toulane and Sierra. The concern in their eyes told me that they knew I was in trouble. But in that moment, Toulane mouthed something. At first I didn't get it, but then it sank in.

Breathe! That was it! I flashed back to the Hearts and Horses kitchen, where I'd reminded Toulane to face her fears by breathing. Now she was doing the same for me.

I smiled and drew in all the sky-blue air my lungs could hold. Then I relaxed my shoulders and blew out the gray—just as my music started up.

Everything suddenly clicked back into place. I didn't need to think. My body knew what to do.

I saluted the judges again and then began. I bounced, hands on hips. With my arms up, I did a straight jump and split jump. I kicked up into a hand-stand and then a forward roll handstand bridge kick-over . . . run and split leap . . . slide and splits. Then, *believing I could do it,* I ran into the round-off back handspring. *Yes!* I struck a pose and finally—with confidence—saluted the judges one last time.

I beamed and drew a deep breath.

A huge wave of applause rose up from the audience. Then I pivoted, head high, and walked off across the mat to join Sierra and Toulane.

"Unbelievable!" Toulane said.

"You were amazing!" Sierra added.

We hugged one another and then watched another gymnast perform. I wasn't just having fun, I was flying high! It must have been contagious, because Toulane and Sierra performed well on floor, too, even though Sierra faltered a little on her landings. By cheering one another on, we'd all become better, more of a true team than ever before. I could see that clearly in our routines.

But the whole time, in the back of my mind, I kept thinking that there were only two open spots— *two spots*—on Shooting Star's level-four competitive team. I didn't want any of us to be left out.

When tryouts ended and scores were being tallied, Toulane, Sierra, and I pulled on our warm-up jackets and then waited on the sidelines.

"No matter what happens," I said, "we're teammates—and friends. Right?"

"Absolutely," Toulane agreed, pulling out her friendship bracelet and putting it on as proof.

Sierra and I did the same, and we caught Josie's attention, pointing at our wrists. She waved back, lifted her arm, and pointed to her wrist, too.

But when I turned back toward Sierra, I noticed her chewing on her lower lip. With only two open spots, I knew she must be fretting about her less-than-perfect landings.

Coach Chip picked up the microphone this time as another coach handed him a list of team scores. We watched for what seemed like forever as he read off scores, club by club. Beaming girls climbed the podium to accept medals. A few clubs took home trophies. As each group stood on the platform, Coach Chip finished his winners' announcements by saying, "Gymnasts salute!"

The crowd cheered as the winning gymnasts lifted their arms high.

"And, finally, for those trying out today for spots on Shooting Star's competitive team . . ." Coach Chip began.

Coach Isabelle handed him a slip of paper.

He listed our order in reverse: "Seventh . . . Sixth . . . Fifth . . . Fourth . . ." The girls from outside our club went up and stood on the lower levels of the podium.

My heart pounded.

Then Coach Chip announced, "Honorable mention and third place goes to . . . Sierra Kuchinko."

Applause sounded as Sierra walked up to accept her team medal. She stood on the podium by Number 3, a hint of disappointment dampening her smile.

"Second place," Coach Chip said, "goes to McKenna Brooks."

It took a moment for the words to register. Then I heard Dad's voice calling, "Way to go, McKenna!" Another round of applause rose up from the crowd as I stepped up and bowed my head to accept my medal.

I'd done it! I'd struggled to come back from my injury, and I'd succeeded. I blinked back tears of relief and joy. I could still barely believe it!

"And first place," Coach Chip said finally, "goes to Toulane Thomas!"

Toulane hurried to climb the podium to my right. Sierra stood to my left. I reached out and squeezed their hands. Then, without being told to do so, we took a bow together. I think we knew that none of us would be standing there without each other.

Coach Chip continued, "A big congratulations, Toulane and McKenna, for earning your positions on Shooting Star's level-four competitive team!"

Coach Chip shook our hands as Coach Isabelle stepped up to the podium. "Congratulations, girls," she said warmly.

As we left the platform, Sierra raced ahead to join her family. I hung back with Toulane, who was standing still. Suddenly, Toulane pulled the medal up and off from around her neck. "Sorry," she whispered to Coach Chip, "but I'm not—" She handed the medal back to Coach Chip. "I just don't want to compete."

Coach Chip looked as if he couldn't believe what he was hearing. Coach Isabelle looked stunned, too. She stepped up alongside Toulane. "Think about what you're doing," said Coach Isabelle. "If you pass on this chance, Sierra will fill your spot."

Tears pooled in Toulane's eyes. "It's what my mom wants," Toulane said in a small voice. "But it's just not . . . it's not what *I* want."

As Toulane's tears spilled over, I reached out and grabbed her hand. "Tell them what you *do* want, Toulane," I whispered.

Toulane shrugged. "I want to have fun again,

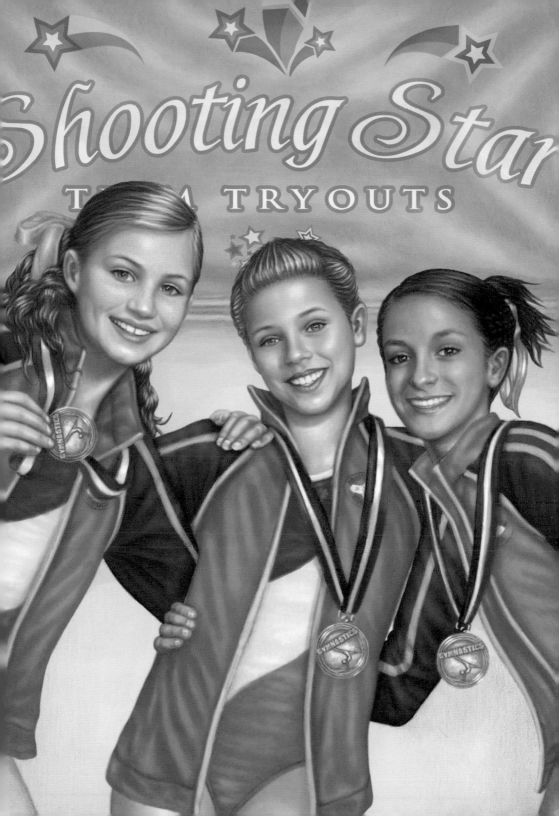

and . . ." She glanced at me. "I really want to do rhythmic gymnastics," she said, sounding more sure of herself. I was proud of her—a little disappointed for me, but happy that Toulane was being honest about what she wanted. That took courage.

Coach Isabelle leaned into Toulane. "Then, Toulane," she said gently, "you need to tell your mom that. She needs to know how you're feeling so that you can make this decision together."

Toulane nodded. "I will," she said.

I gave Toulane one more hug—long and strong. As I watched her walk away, I didn't know what to hope for. I'd miss Toulane on the competitive team, but I'd be happy for her, too, if she quit to follow her own dream. And I'd be happy for Sierra, whose own dream of making the team could come true.

I could barely believe all that had happened.

I'd made the team . . .

I'd made the team.

I'd made the team!

Monday night, it was finally time to celebrate my success at the Space Needle with Josie, Toulane, Mom, and Dad.

We met up in front of the Needle with Josie, who got front-door service when her parents dropped her off with their van.

"I've never been up to the top before," Josie said. "I can't wait!"

"I have," Toulane said. "It's incredible! But I've never been to the restaurant before."

We entered the towering building and checked in at the counter. A man in a top hat greeted us: "Welcome to the Space Needle!"

Then he gave us a buzzing device. "Take the elevator to the top," he said. "Explore the observation deck. And when your buzzer goes off, head down one level to the SkyCity Restaurant. Enjoy!"

This wasn't an *ordinary* elevator. The elevator operator told us that it held up to 25 people and that when we reached the observation deck, we'd have climbed 520 feet.

My stomach dropped as the elevator sped upward. When the doors opened, we stepped out into light-speckled darkness. Stars winked overhead, and lights glittered all around below.

As Mom and Dad walked, hand in hand, around the circular deck, Josie wheeled beside me and Toulane.

I leaned against the railing and searched the pinpoint lights of Seattle below. "Over there!" I said, pointing into the speckled darkness. "That's our neighborhood."

Toulane and Josie looked out over the railing, following my gaze. Then Josie glanced upward. "I feel like I can almost touch the stars," she said wistfully.

"Me, too," Toulane said, leaning on the railing, head back.

She looked so relaxed that I had to ask, "Toulane, how did it go with your mom? Is she going to let you quit the team?"

Toulane shook her head back and forth and then up and down. "It wasn't pretty at first," she said. "But when Mom finally saw that I was working toward a dream I didn't want anymore—well, things went much better. She said she had no idea I was so unhappy." Toulane shrugged. "I guess I should have said something sooner."

I felt a rush of happiness for Toulane and then a pang of sadness, too, for me. "Toulane," I said, "I'm going to miss you being with me on the team."

"I will, too," she said. "But we'll be at the gym together when I start taking rhythmic gymnastics. And a lot will be the same. We'll all still be friends," she said, glancing first at me and then at Josie.

I smiled back. Everything was working out.

Yesterday, I'd gone to Hearts and Horses to talk with Shannon. We came up with a schedule of my helping out for two hours every *other* week. It was possible to do both gymnastics and volunteering, with a little creativity. I'd gotten used to balancing the two, and I didn't want to give up either one.

I glanced back up at the stars overhead. For a few more moments, I enjoyed simply being side by side with Toulane and Josie. I breathed in the cool, damp air and then gazed across the sound at the mountains beyond.

When the reservation buzzer vibrated in my hand, I jumped, which made my friends giggle. "Time to eat," I announced.

We took the elevator one level down to the restaurant and stepped out into a small lobby. A woman in a belted black dress greeted us and led us through the amber glow of candles on tabletops. "Enjoy," she said, motioning us to our table, right beside a circular wall of glass panels.

Mom and Dad must have let them know that Josie was coming, because the waiter had already moved a chair away so that Josie could easily slide in with her wheelchair. I squeezed Mom's hand.

"Oh," Josie said seconds after we sat down. "I can tell that we're moving!"

The motion was slow, but the whole dining room floor revolved around the restaurant's kitchen and lobby.

"This place is awesome!" Toulane said, staring out the window.

I couldn't stop smiling. "It's amazing," I agreed.

"You *girls* are the amazing ones," Dad said. "so let's celebrate your success." He lifted his water glass. "A toast to an amazing student—and tutor— who have made excellent progress since the start of school!"

I smiled at Josie, and we all lifted our glasses. *Clink. Clink. Clink.*

"And," added Mom, "to two hardworking gymnasts, who have helped make each other better!"

Clink. Clink. Clink.

After a delicious dinner of crab macaroni and cheese, I caught sight of our waiter, carrying a dessert on a silver platter. "Look!" I said, pointing.

"I believe this is for you girls—to share," the waiter said, setting the dessert down in the middle of the table.

The silver bowl was filled with what looked like a mound of whipped cream topped with a cherry. Then the waiter performed some kind of magic and poured something into the base of the silver bowl. The whole thing started billowing. White clouds of fog lifted from the dessert and rolled across the table.

Josie laughed out loud.

"Cool!" Toulane said, trying to catch some of the white fog in her hands.

"Is it alive?" Dad joked.

We oohed and aahed and then each lifted a spoon to try the dessert.

"Mmmm!" Josie said. "Hot fudge and vanilla ice cream. My favorite!"

Toulane laughed. "Mine too," she said.

"And mine," I agreed, reminded again that no matter all the ways my friends and I are different, we sure have lots in common.

The fog spilling from around the dessert

gradually slowed and disappeared.

"Gray sky out?" Toulane asked, meeting my eyes.

"Definitely *out*," I said, scooping another spoonful of ice cream and hot fudge.

"And having fun together?" Josie added.

I beamed. "Definitely . . . *in*."

Letter from American Girl

Dear Readers,

    McKenna is a determined girl who uses her strengths to overcome challenges—and who encourages others to do the same.

    Here are the stories of five real girls helped their friends, siblings, and other children overcome challenges. These girls set—and met—great goals with a little creativity and a *lot* of determination.

    We hope you are inspired by these stories. *Every* girl has the power to aim high and to help others believe in themselves, too.

                 Your friends at American Girl

365 HATS

Snowboarding champion Katie W. used her passion for a snowy sport to help a friend. "When I snowboard, I feel like I'm floating through the air," says the 13-year-old Wisconsin girl. "It's my happy place." But Katie felt awful when she found out that Gina, a friend from school, had cancer. Gina was fighting for her life. She also was worried about losing her hair during chemotherapy treatment.

To help Gina feel more confident about how she looked, Katie decided to collect 365 colorful snowboarding hats. "That way, she could feel good about how she looked every day of the year," says Katie. She also got out her crochet hook and started making colorful hats decorated with pom-poms and patterns. She wrote to snowboard companies and sporting groups to ask for hat donations. She also set up collection bins at her snowboarding competitions.

Soon, boxes of hats began to arrive—more than 500 hats so far. "Wearing the hats made Gina less afraid of being bald," says Katie. With more than enough hats, Katie and Gina began sending hats to children's cancer units at hospitals around the country.

It wasn't long before Gina's chemotherapy was finished. "She's much better now," says Katie, who is still collecting and donating hats to other kids. "I was really glad to help."

A LAW—PASSED!

Grace G. got her first pair of hearing aids when she was three months old, and she has worn them ever since. Hearing aids don't make her hearing perfect—they make all sounds louder, not just the sounds she wants to hear. She had to learn how to concentrate on the important sounds and ignore the rest.

Grace, age 10, doesn't let her hearing loss get in the way. She takes dance lessons and does gymnastics and cheerleading. "Lots of times I forget that I'm wearing hearing aids," she says, "but they're important to me." Grace got hearing aids so that she could learn to speak, which is hard to do if you don't know what words sound like.

Still, not all kids who experience hearing loss are able to get hearing aids. Hearing aids are expensive, and many insurance companies won't pay for them. Grace and her mom spent a lot of time at their state capitol, trying to convince lawmakers to write a law that would make insurance companies pay for hearing aids for kids. Finally the law passed—and it was named after Grace!

"The law will help kids in my state get the hearing aids they need," says Grace. "I feel so proud about that."

BEADING TO BEAT AUTISM

Michala R.'s little brother, Evan, has autism, a disorder that makes it difficult for him to communicate and control himself. But things got better after 8-year-old Evan started a new kind of medical treatment. "Evan doesn't have as many temper tantrums," says Michala, age 12. "Now if I call his name, he looks at me, and unlike before, he laughs and plays."

When Michala heard that the hospital needed $200,000 for autism research, she started making and selling bracelets with colorful beads. She sold them for three dollars each, and she called her effort "Beading to Beat Autism."

Soon, word of the project spread, and Michala couldn't make bracelets fast enough. She handed out kits of supplies so that others could help. Through bracelet sales and cash donations, Michala raised $200,000 in just six months. The money helped doctors learn more about the treatment that helped Evan—which meant they might be able to help other kids, too.

Michala is now working on a plan to raise $300 million to fund an autism center in her hometown. It's a big task, but Michala is confident. "If you know you can achieve your goal, then you will," she says. "My motto is, 'You gotta believe.'"

TWO HEARTS FOR HAITI

Ruthie was adopted from Haiti. When she heard about an earthquake in Haiti, she wanted to cry. "I was worried about all of the people in Haiti, a lot of them kids like me," she says.

Raegan is Ruthie's closest friend, and when she learned of the earthquake, she knew right away that she wanted to help. Raegan decided to swim laps to raise money for people in Haiti.

She asked people to pledge money to go toward Haiti if she met her goal of swimming 150 laps—more than two miles!

"I knew it would be tough," says Raegan, "but Ruthie inspired me to try my hardest. She said, 'Raegan, just believe in yourself.'"

It took Raegan an hour and 17 minutes to swim 150 laps, but she did it—and raised much more money than she thought she would. When a doctor in Florida heard about her swim, he offered to double the donations. "We sent about $70,000 to Haiti," says Raegan. "It's buying food and fixing buildings. It's paying for medicine—lots of things."

The friends' next project? Raising money to build a school in Haiti. Ruthie says the school would be "a dream come true," and the girls are determined to make it happen—together.

Mary Casanova loves to read, but it wasn't always that way. Though she was good at reading aloud in class, she struggled to comprehend much of what she read. She loved to check out books at the library, but as an "active, can't-sit-still, adventure-seeking kid," she found *finishing* books difficult.

Now, as the author of over two dozen books for young readers—including *Cécile, Jess, Chrissa,* and *Chrissa Stands Strong* for American Girl—she's passionate about writing stories that kids can't put down.

When Mary isn't writing—or traveling for research or to speak at schools and conferences—she's likely reading a good book, hiking with her husband and three dogs, or horseback riding in the north woods of Minnesota.